S

Flipping the lock and deadbolt on the front door, I shuffle to the side so Gunz can shove a chair back underneath the handle for added security.

"Did you lock the screen door?" he asks, double checking the chair legs will catch on the floor, preventing any intrusion.

I nod, dusting my hands on my thighs. "Yep. Did you secure the back door?"

"Of course, what do you take me for, a novice?" He winks, pulling a Dum Dum from the inside pocket of his cut. Peeling off the wrapper, he presses its sugary goodness to my lips. I grin before popping it inside my mouth. Gunz does the same for himself, opting for a festive holiday flavor—gingerbread, I think.

The song on Pandora's Christmas station, which blasts through a wireless speaker in the living room courtesy of Gunz, swaps to Jingle Bell Rock as we get back to work. It's the Saturday after Thanksgiving and I paid off four of the brothers to take my big ole Grinch out tonight, as far away from the house as humanly possible. Ya see, the old man is *not* a fan of

3

the holidays. And when I say he doesn't like Christmas, this isn't an exaggeration. We're talking, he shits on all things holly or jolly this time of the year. When I was a kid he once tore down all the decorations I made from the walls in the clubhouse. A week later, he spent an entire day taking me shopping to make up for his Ebenezer ways. Yet, he never fails in ruining something or other.

Unboxing the new garland I bought last week and hid, I hand it up to Gunz who's standing on a chair in the kitchen. Using Command strips, he secures the berry-filled awesomeness to the top edge of the cedar cupboards. I want every square inch of Big's house— our house—covered in Christmas flair. I opted for a simple silver and red theme, not wanting it to be too gaudy. Honestly, I was tempted to decorate in bright variants of pink, when a responsible Jez stepped in and talked me out of it. Something about gender neutral and not giving Big a fucking coronary. Little does she know this is enough to make him shit asteroid-sized bricks.

Have I mentioned my man has never decorated his house before?

No?

Well, he hasn't. Not once. However, he might have told me I could put a small tree in our daughter's bedroom, as a compromise. *Ha.* Laughable, right? *But,* I wasn't allowed to do anything else. You think I listened? Fuck no. That's why Gunz is here as backup. We're on decorating duty. I was even tempted to invite the sisters to help. Then again, I didn't think they should be subjected to Big whenever he comes home. Nobody deserves that. Not even me, or our kid. That's why Harley's in bed. Plus, it's past her bedtime. Grandpa Gunz gave her a lavender-scented bath and rocked her to sleep while I set up the nine-foot pre-lit tree in the corner of the living room, close to the stone fireplace. I've already swagged it out with ribbon and loaded on expensive ornaments; courtesy of the devil that is Pinterest and its endless ideas.

Swaying my hips to the music, clad in a pair of Frosty pajamas and my red-and-white candy striped socks, I unbox the bulb shaped candles for the center of the table.

This is the life. When I lived by myself, I never cared much for holiday decor. I did a small tree and a few knickknacks. Now that it's Harley's first Christmas, I'll be damned if our house doesn't kick ass. Christmas spirit is in full force 'round here. Jez has an entire Nativity scene on her lawn. Big has a habit of kicking the Three Wise Men down any chance he can get. See, I told you he's an asshole. Even Mickey and Gypsy have those white wire reindeer in their yard, and Pixie's got a blow-up Mickey Mouse wearing a Santa costume.

Finished with the garland, Gunz hops off the chair humming to Little Drummer Boy now playing on the radio. He saunters into the living room, digs out his pocket knife and flips it open with his thumb. Kicking the second of three tree boxes away from the wall, he slices the tape in one smooth motion. Before I'm done arranging the centerpiece, he has half of the box's guts on the floor.

"Whoa," I call out, plucking my sucker stick from my mouth. "Hold up. That's the basement tree."

Gunz's brows furrow deep in thought, lifting another piece and fanning it out on the floor. "I thought this was the bedroom tree."

Damn. Maybe he's right.

Tossing the empty candle box in a giant, black bag along with my Dum Dum trash, I kneel beside the opened tree box to read the label, trying to recall what my plan was. I purchased three new trees for our place. Now I can't remember if I got this one for the basement or not. One is white and the other black. I know what you're thinking... *A black Christmas tree, really, Bink?*

Yes. *Really.*

It's *only* seven foot. A full foot shorter than the white with clear lights. I've never been a fan of colored lights on trees. Too much clashing with their ornament counterparts. I know, you're rolling your eyes because I'm *that* kind of decorator. Maybe in a few years I won't care about matchy-matchy shit. This year isn't that year. Harley isn't old enough to make her own ornaments, and Big would've trashed any bulbs he was gifted before... He's an *asshole*, remember?

"The black might clash with the red walls in the basement," Gunz notes, shrugging off his cut and draping it over the arm of the nearest couch.

Has he lost his mind at his advanced age? The Sacred Sinners are red and black.

I look up at him from the floor, brows knitting together. "What do you mean it clashes? Red and black look fine together. It would clash more in our bedroom." Around my birthday this year I bought new bedding, repainted the walls, and styled our bedrooms. As in plural. We have two. One upstairs and the other in the basement. Or have you forgotten already?

Gunz taps a red and black tat on his forearm then

rolls his eyes and smirks fondly, like he wants to wrap me in a giant hug 'cause he adores the hell outta me. "I know. I was bein' sarcastic. Does my sarcasm not register with this music playing?"

Butthead.

I stick out my tongue and snort at his dry humor. "I'll have you know, Christmas music is ah-mazing." It really is.

"If you say so." The smirk grows to a full on grin. A flash of white teeth peeks through those lips surrounded in a gray goatee.

Covering my mouth, I mock gasp, eyes flying wide. "You did not just insult Christmas music in this house."

He chuckles. It's jolly like Santa himself. "Pretty sure Big has never had a lick of fuckin' Christmas music playin' in this place ever."

Another fake gasp from me, playing up my shock to the next level as I clutch a branch of the tree. "You sayin' I popped its Christmas cherry?"

"In all ways, yeah. So let's keep takin' its virginity. Make it *goood*." A short laugh and charming smile is delivered from my second favorite guy in the world. Okay, perhaps he's my favorite favorite. Big can come in second. He hates Christmas after all. Gunz can win. Not like I have to tell the old man that. Don't wanna make his grumpy ass jealous.

"Let's take it nice and slow so the house can savor our fancy fucking," I suggest.

Gunz's head cocks to the side, eyes on mine. "What the hell is fancy fucking, Baby Doll?"

I shrug, both shoulders inches from touching earlobes. "I dunno. When you decorate it in pretty stuff ultimately bringing it closer to orgasm?"

"Whatever you—" Pausing mid-sentence, Gunz extracts the phone from his back pocket and reads a text. As he does this, I get back to work. This black tree isn't gonna set itself up.

Scooping the pieces back inside the box, I shove the tree toward the basement door. Skirting around the long rectangle, I open said door and grip the lip of the cardboard flap, yanking it closer to the steps. Poised on the top stair, I position the tree at the right angle and let the bitch slide its way to the basement. What? Don't look at me like that. I'm improvising. Who wants to carry a heavy box down a flight of stairs? Crazy people, that's who. I'm not *that* crazy. Are you?

Following the tree down, I kick the last bit when it gets stuck, and nudge it further with my socked toe once it's cleared the steps. The living space down here isn't as large as upstairs, but it has plenty of room for a festive tree. Knowing exactly where it goes, I maneuver the box closer to the corner where it will fit and not obstruct the walkways, couch, or the kitchen area. I crouch and tear open the box. It doesn't take long to have the pieces spread out, ready to assemble. Isn't it weird how much tree designs have changed over the past decades? When I was a kid, we had all these individual branches you had to hook into the stand by color. If the paint they dipped the metal tip in wore off you had to hope you got them right by size. They were abrasive and left rashes on your forearms when you fanned them out before stringing lights. These pre-lit babies are genius. Easy out, easy up, easy takedown. No muss, little fuss. I wish they'd had these when I was a child. My parents didn't do much for the holidays. Mom was too caught up in her own crap, but we did always have a tree. Sometimes it was real. Most of the time it was fake. I've never cared one way or the other. A tree is a tree. And real ones can be messy. Big would hate that more than he's going to hate this. That's why I opted for artificial. It's less hassle. We also have a little one and Pretzel to consider. He hasn't experienced a real tree either. The last thing I want is him or Harley eating the needles.

"We've got company!" Gunz hollers down the stairs.

Shit.

"What kind of company?!" On a mission, I quickly assemble the four-legged tree stand and stack the bottom layer of black branches on by sliding them into the post to lock them in place.

Please say it's Jez. Please say it's Jez.

"He's back."

Dammit!

Those jerks, they didn't keep him out long enough. I've got two trees left to decorate and our stockings to hang. I'm gonna kill Viper. He knew how important this was. This is why I should've sent Gunz. He would've stolen Big's bike keys, if necessary. Fuckin' pussies. *Gah!*

Not letting my man win, I piece the black tree together row by row without stopping. "I'm not done."

"I know."

"Stall him. Please."

The doorbell rings. When nobody answers in less than a second, Big pounds on the door. Mighty, impatient blows that don't let up.

Gunz shuts down the music, and I abandon my

work with an exhausted sigh to deal with a pissed-off old man. This should be fun.

As soon as I reach the top step I hear him bellowing, "Bink!"

"Hold your horses!" Irritated to the nth degree, I stomp to the front door refusing to open it before I'm done. He can come back later like he was supposed to in the first place.

Gunz leans his shoulder against the wall watching the entry and me, as I approach. The windowpanes in the door are rattling. Could he knock any freaking louder? Doesn't he know we have a sleeping baby here?

"Bink! Open this fucking door!"

"No! You need to calm down."

"What're you doin' in there? Why is this door locked? Why aren't you answering my texts?" he rattles off, impatient with my lack of follow through.

"I'm busy. Come back later."

"What the fu— Busy doin' what?"

"None of your business."

"It's my damn house."

"No. It's our house," I snark.

"Fine. Our. House. What is goin' on in *our* house?"

Smartass.

"I said I'm busy. You weren't supposed to be home

yet."

"Well excuse me for missin' my old lady."

Whatever.

"That's not why you're here, Big. Don't pretend like it is."

"The hell it ain't." He has the audacity to sound offended.

I roll my eyes.

When I don't comment he starts in again. "Sugar Tits."

"Who diss?" I act dumb.

Yes, I realize I'm a total butthole. I could stop this entire thing by opening the door and letting him inside. But I don't want to. Nothing good will come of it. He's already angry, and I'm not finished with my Christmas decorating extravaganza.

"Christ, woman! What're you doin' in there?"

"Who diss?" I glance over my shoulder to look at Gunz who's smirking at my idiocy. Whoever said picking on Big wasn't fun? It's a blast.

"We're not playin' a game. I asked you a question," he growls, not amused in the least.

I trace the edge of the cold windowpane with my finger. "And I said come back later. You're home too early. I'm not finished." There, I toned it down a notch. I can play nice... sometimes.

An eerie silence descends, and I start to wonder if he's left. Too bad I know him better than that. Nothing is ever that easy with Big.

There's a crash at the back door and thundering footfalls as my damn man breaks into our house. I turn around and deliver a withering glare to Gunz who was supposed to secure the rear door.

"What the hell?" I hiss.

Gunz shrugs a shoulder, not the least bit upset as he pulls a sucker from his jeans pocket and pops it into his maw. He's lucky I adore him because this is about to be one epic showdown. Grab your front row seats boys and girls.

Big stomps through the kitchen hard enough that the leftover dishes in the sink rattle. "What the fuck!" he booms when he notices the decorations. Screeching to a growly halt by the cupboards he glares at the offending garland. A breath later he reaches up and rips the entire strip of greenery down. Then chucks it onto the floor where he stomps on it like an overgrown child. This is ridiculous.

"What the hell do you think you're doing?" I approach him, stopping a few feet short on the threshold of the living room.

Big scans my body up and down, noticing my

Christmas jammies. "You decorated." His upper lip snarls the words.

Hip cocked to the side, arms crossed over my chest, I jerk a nod. "I decorated."

"I said no." To cement this declaration Big grinds his boot heel into the once beautiful garland. He's gonna pay for that later. That greenery wasn't cheap. I picked it specifically for our kitchen. He's gonna rue the day he pissed me off. Ebenezer Scrooge won't win this one.

"Well, I'm in this relationship, too. And I said yes," I snap.

Leaning his own hip against the counter, Big crosses those massive arms over his pecs, trying to appear intimidating. If only that worked on me. It doesn't. I'm immune. "We compromised."

I shake my head violently, lips pursed. "No. You dictated. *You*. There was no compromise."

"I gave you a tree in Leech's room. That's a compromise."

"No. That's a load of controlling bullshit, is what that is."

Big two-finger points to the ornamented tree in our living room, appalled. "*That* is not staying here."

"Then neither am I."

"What's that supposed to mean?" He glares.

"That means... I understand that you hate Christmas. But I will not let you ruin our daughter's first one because of *your* issues. Not hers, Big. *Yours*. Last time I checked, we're not Jehovah's Witnesses. We're allowed to celebrate holidays however we see fit. If that means I move me and our daughter out of this house for December, then so be it."

"You can't mean that." The wind's been knocked from his sails as he frowns.

"Oh. I do." His bedroom at the clubhouse is a fine alternative.

Big scrubs a hand over his head. "You can't leave me. You're mine."

I sigh, not wanting to make this worse than it already is. "I'm not leaving you, silly. I'm respecting your stupid fucking wishes and staying elsewhere for the holidays."

"Without me," he mumbles, frown deepening into sullen baby territory.

"Yes. Without you." This guy does seasonal bike runs for Toys for Tots to collect Christmas presents, but he can't stand the holiday. He's a conundrum, my man.

"'Cause I hate Christmas?"

"I don't care what you hate. But I don't like when

it affects our daughter's future happiness. She isn't gonna be the kid who doesn't get to have decorations in the house or celebrate Christmas because you can't stand it. That's unfair. It's my duty to protect her, even if it's from her own father's ridiculousness."

"Her. Own. Father? It's *my* duty to protect her, Sugar Tits. Not yours."

I'm not gonna touch that machismo with a ten-foot pole. "Do you seriously not want her waking up to Santa's presents under the tree on Christmas morning?"

Big tosses his hands up in exasperation, before returning them to their home below those yummy pecs. "Why do you think I said to put up a tree in her bedroom?"

Oy vey. This man.

"That's not enough, and you know it."

"So instead of easin' me into this, you decide to turn our house into Christmas fucking Wonderland? I say one thing, and you do the polar opposite."

Alright, I admit it, he has a point. A tiny one. Itty bitty. It's so small it might as well be microscopic. The size of an amoeba. I could've gone with an average tree and some stockings. The stockings didn't have to be custom black with white monograms.

What can I say? Following stupid directions has never been my strong suit.

As cool as ice I shrug one shoulder. "Christmas is supposed to look like Christmas. So yeah, I bought three trees." Let's see what he has to say about that. I also purchased lawn ornaments and an oversized snow globe with Santa riding a motorcycle inside it, among other holiday-themed decorations I found at the store.

Big's nostrils flare, cheeks flaming red. "Three. Fucking. Trees?"

"Yes. A white one, green one, and black one." I count them off for emphasis. Might as well be honest. He's gonna find out anyhow.

"Where were you gonna put these damn trees?"

Up your tight ass if you don't watch your tone.

"Living room." I raise my pointer finger, visibly counting like a sarcastic bitch. "Basement." Up goes a second, my middle digit. "Bedroom." I finish with a third.

He smashes his lips together. They disappear momentarily as he curtails the outburst I know is simmering below the surface. He wants to yell at me, put his foot down, create a bigger scene; yet, he's no moron. Big knows if he unleashes that foulness it won't end well for him. "Which bedroom? You'd better say Leech's." Those back teeth grit together. His throat taut with restrained fury.

"Ours," I blurt, nudging him an inch further to the breaking point.

"What. The. Fuck? Come on, babe. You're pushin' it here. Green shit over the cupboards. Ugly candle-lookin' shit on the table. The tree—" Those pissed-off blue eyes shift to the living room.

"Don't," I warn.

"...is ugly," he finishes with a smug smile, single dimple and all. Stupid asshole.

Agitated, I flip him the bird and rub the sentiment against my temple, down the side of my face, and across my lips like I'm applying lipstick before I reprimand the Grinchy bastard. "Fuck you. It's not ugly. If I had my way, it'd be pink and black."

"That'd still be ugly."

Gah! This is why nobody will win. Time to change tactics.

"Why do you hate Christmas so much?"

"That's not up for discussion." A growl.

Always with the brush-off. It's fine and dandy to talk about certain things. Big's past, not so much. Over the years I've learned bits and pieces of what went down before I was born. Little tidbits I'd be fed like a dog does treats. Enough to keep you content, but never enough to slake your voracious appetite. But there are gaps. Huge ones.

"Yes, it is, if you expect me to tone it down," I return in a less growly manner than him.

"There is no expecting. It's gonna happen. End of story. A tree in Leech's room and... a stocking for her... only."

"Well, that's just too damn bad because I already bought us each a stocking." Even got an L one for Harley, to pacify her daddy and the ridiculous nickname he's given her... which has unfortunately stuck. Figured if I got a B on mine and a B on Big's, it was only fair. Would've bought everyone else stockings had it been necessary. Gunz still has the one I made him with gold puff paint when I was in second grade. I'd made one for Big around then, but I'm not sure what he did with it. It probably ended up in the trash.

"That's not my problem. You're not puttin' 'em up," he argues, failing epically.

"Yes. I am." On the fireplace mantel.

"Then don't be surprised when they end up in the garbage."

I two-finger point at his giant six-foot-eight form. "If you ruin one more thing I paid for with my money,

I'll chop your nuts off." Those digits pause their aim at his jean-clad crotch, where that impressive cock sleeps.

Big smirks as if he finds me adorably funny. "If you do that, I can't get hard. Which means no more dick for you."

"You think I'd want your dick after this?"

A comical eyebrow arches. "You sayin' you don't?"

"You're gonna end up with ED soon enough anyhow, at your advanced age. Might as well start the process early." Not the nicest thing to hit below the belt with, but he's insufferable, and I'm gonna win this argument fair and square.

That smirk washes clean off Big's unshaven face, expression twisting into an unimpressed sneer. "I am not gonna get ED."

"You're fifty-one. Any day now and he's gonna be a soldier who's laid to rest. No more pussy salutes." There's some truth to what I'm saying. He might be lucky and have a fully functioning pecker for his age. But there is gonna come a time it's not gonna work.

"Will you stop talkin' about my cock like that?"

Touchy touchy.

"I'll stop talkin' about your dick if you..." Refusing to give him a chance to contest what I'm about to demand, I approach the beast, loop my finger through a belt loop that's also occupied with his bike chain belt, and attempt to drag the stubborn ox into the living room. He doesn't budge, and let's be real, I can't force Big to follow suit if he isn't otherwise inclined. I don't have that much physical power. I'm short. He's more than a foot taller and much heavier. I'm also not pregnant anymore so I can't cry about maybe hurting the baby should I strain myself. And I can't use Pretzel to threaten the stubborn man, because our dog sleeps with Harley. It's gonna take more than us bickering to coax Pretzel away from her bedside. Basically, I'm fucked.

"What're you doin', Sugar Tits?" Big chuckles, thoroughly enjoying my pathetic struggle.

"Christ. Come. On," I grit, trying once more to yank him forth to no stinking avail. My feet slip and slide across the kitchen flooring, doing fuck-all to gain traction or move this Neanderthal. I spin around to face him, line both of my stocking-covered feet with his massive booted ones, toes to toes, and hook another finger through a belt loop—one on either side of his Sacred Sinners buckle. Then I lean back, using all of my weight to make him step away from the counter he's leaning on, even if it's a mere inch.

Nada.

Dammit. This ain't gonna work. I'm either gonna rip his jeans or fall flat on my ass. Neither solves a thing.

"Big," I whine, getting frustrated with my lack of size and his refusal. "Come on."

Big grips my forearms, to steady me. "Babe, you're gonna fall, and I'm not movin' 'til you tell me what the hell it is you're up to."

"Stop fighting me. Just come."

"Come where?"

"In the living room."

"I don't wanna come in the living room, I wanna come in your mouth."

"Jesus Christ. Do you ever not think about sex?"

"Are you my old lady?"

"Yes," I clip, staring daggers at the infuriating biker.

"There's your answer. I'm never gonna stop thinkin' about sex when I'm around your fine ass." Big flicks his eyes to his zipper, and that's when I notice a wet stain has begun to grow, darkening the denim. His budding erection flexes as if it's showing off for its mate. Of course, he's excited at a time like this. We argue, he's hard. We don't argue, he's hard. If I haven't showered in days, shaven my legs or pussy in three weeks, or brushed my teeth in eighteen hours, he's still raring to go. There's no such thing as dick repellent in this household. It's weird. You'd think my unkempt hair and unflattering pajamas would be a deterrent. If anything, I gotta wonder if the *mom vibe* doesn't fuel that incessant libido. Not that I'm much better. He's hot as sin. Who wouldn't wanna ride that dick? Don't answer that, you sex fiend. It's a rhetorical question. I don't wanna have to go crazy bitch on your ass for wanting to play hide the bratwurst with my old man. Sometimes keeping your desires to yourself is a good thing. You don't get cut. Capiche?

Now... where was I? Oh, right, the living room.

"Big, it's time to bring you and your boner to the couch."

His head tilts, a smirk stretching until a flash of white peeks between those full lips. "What's the magic word?"

"I'll let you fuck me?" *Tomorrow.*

"Well, alrighty then. That works. Lead the way, hot stuff."

Men, always thinking with their tiny penis brains.

Unhooking one finger, I use the other to drag Ebenezer to one of our black leather couches. I position him in front before shoving that beefy chest, and down he drops onto the cushions. They groan in protest as the leather forms to his impressive backside. Knowing he won't sit there for too long without an incentive, I straddle his lap and lock my fingers behind his neck. His low ponytail tickles the backs of my fingers as Big settles his paws on my plump ass cheeks.

"This is nice." Leaning in, he nips my bottom lip. "I like you on me." To cement that thought, Big uses his strength to grind my pussy against his straining erection. It nudges my clit on the first try sending fireworks of pleasure through my core, turning me on. The bastard.

That's not how this is gonna work. We've got a Christmas debate to handle.

Sex can come later, if I'm not pissed. If I am, he can suffer from a case of blue balls. At least we didn't have to ask Gunz to leave. He must've slipped out when we were fighting.

"Tell me why you don't like Christmas." I dive straight in before my hormones win and I'm stuck with no agreement and a pussy full of cum.

"Is this why you brought me over here, to coerce me into tellin' you shit I already said is not up for discussion? Using your pussy as bait?" He spanks my ass to show me how much of a bad girl I've been, then grips both globes, kneading the flesh. I bite back a groan. My eyelids flutter as I drop my forehead to his shoulder, getting a headful of his intoxicating scent: man, wind, leather, and spice. *Damn.* Why do I love him so much? This shouldn't be foreplay, yet is. The sting radiates through my backside, followed by an ache. A deep, sensual one that awakens certain parts of my anatomy that need to stay asleep for a little while longer.

I refrain from answering his questions. They're rhetorical anyhow. He knows I use my assets to my advantage. Who wouldn't? Just as he knows by spanking me, I'm growing wetter by the second. "If you want me to concede a little, you gotta do the same," I mumble to his throat, lips brushing there, reveling in his warm pulse as it beats against them.

A lighter spank is delivered. It's more like a firm pat. "You gonna throw the decorations out if I tell you?" Big nuzzles the side of my head with his nose, eliciting a shiver.

Two can play at that game. I unthread my hands from behind Big's neck and drag them down the front of his chest to the hem of his shirt. Big sucks in a sharp breath as I dip underneath, smoothing my palms up the warm, hard slab of his stomach. "No.

But I'll... not set up the bedroom Christmas tree. If you tell me enough to make me understand, maybe I'll even give up a couple other decorations." Leaning in closer, I lick from shoulder to ear, where I pause to nibble his lobe between my teeth. Not enough to make him moan, but enough to make his balls feel it—the need to unload. To win, I'm willing to play dirty.

"Wh-what about the living room tree?" Big croaks, as a shudder rushes through him, fingers digging into my ass. There'll be bruises tomorrow.

"That's non-negotiable," I husk, laving my tongue across his deliciously salty throat.

Big wraps his palm around the base of my neck, asserting his dominance. And I let him. Just as I let him carefully pull my head backward, forcing me to garner eye contact. "The hell it is," he grates as my blues delve into his heated ones, fusing hot and heavy. There's a neediness simmering beneath the hardtack surface, as hunger swirls in the depths which we both feel, yet refuse to confess. I want him as much as he wants me. But what I want more is to win this Christmas showdown. Attaining the upper hand against a man who always wins in other facets of his life, beyond the scope of our relationship; I wrap his hot body, heart, and soul around my pinkie finger. Stubbornness might be Big's middle name, but Bink's the name he moans as he licks my pussy night after night. The name he's claimed as his. He might be the president of the Sacred Sinners Motorcycle Club—feared and revered by many, but to me, he's mine. I own him. And as fate has decreed, he owns a little bit of me, too.

Tracing shapes across his abs with my fingertips, I cup his face with my other hand. The graying scruff abrades my palm in the sexiest of ways. "It's for Harley. Don't take this from her," I plead in the softest voice.

"Fine." He sighs. "I can survive the tree. But those bulb candle things on the table have got to fuckin' go."

See? Progress.

I brush my thumb over the sharp edge of his jaw. "Agreed."

"And don't go overboard in the clubhouse either. I know you well enough. If you give shit up here, you'll make it throw up elsewhere. That's not the deal. If I compromise, you have to agree not to do your deceitful woman shit and truly meet me halfway."

If I wanted to spend the entire holiday season fighting him tooth and nail, I'd do what he claims.

However, I want this to be special. I want us to make our own traditions. That's the goal. Not fighting, even if that often leads to fucking. Delicious hate fucking. Last week, in the clubhouse kitchen, I'd snapped at him for something or other, and ended up bent over the counter with a dick in my pussy. This old lady stuff is hard business, I tell ya. So *hard*.

"I won't," I vow and mean it. "Just a few decorations, a tree, and a chair for Santa at the clubhouse." *And mistletoe over every doorway.*

Those perfect eyebrows jump to his hairline. "Santa, really?"

"Gunz already agreed to play the part."

Big's eyes roll, lips thinning. "Of course, he did."

I pat his cheek in mock discipline. Just because he's the Grinch, doesn't mean Gunz has to be. "Don't hate. He wants to give Harley the best first Christmas. And the other kids a nice one, too. It's not just about us. It's about Jez's kids, Debbie's. This is also our nephew's first Christmas, in case you forgot."

"I know." Dropping his head back, resting it on the top of the couch, Big sighs long and hard as if this is killing him to concede. "You weren't here last year. We didn't get to spend Christmas together," he complains to the ceiling.

Leaning forward, I drag my pillow-soft lips across the span of his throat. "I know, babe," I whisper there, kissing the hollow at the base before delving the tip of my tongue inside to sample. *Mmmm... more Big...* my favorite.

A rumble of pleasure percolates in that muscled chest.

Testing the band of my pajama bottoms, Big slips his hand into them and my panties, to palm my bare ass. "I didn't like that shit."

"Me, either. Is that why you're extra salty about it this year?"

"A little... But you know I had a shit childhood. Boss Man didn't think I was worthy of presents. The club whores always gave me something." A shrug.

My poor poor man.

"And your mom wasn't around." A statement, because that's something I know is true.

A stiff nod. "Right."

"You know you deserve love."

Grunt.

"I love you."

He swallows hard.

"A lot," I add.

"Yeah." Big's voice cracks, throat working.

To tear him from whatever unpleasantness

brewing inside that thick skull of his, I rock against Big's waning cock to wake it back up. Our lives aren't perfect. Our love isn't perfect. Hell, it's stressful as shit sometimes. We bicker a lot. The club always comes first, and that can take its toll. Especially when he can't share things with me that eat at him. His past isn't an open book. I've accepted that. What I don't like is him letting that past rule our family's future. Harley can't carry her father's baggage any more than I should have to carry my own father's.

"I want you inside me," I whisper against the hollow of his throat.

"Fuck." Big slips a hand deeper inside my panties. Two fingers part my soaked folds. "Fuuuck," he moans, noticing how wet I am for him. The digits swirl around my entrance before one dives home, impaling me in a single, delicious thrust.

I groan low and achy, relishing the invasion, eyes falling shut. Teeth sink into my bottom lip as he fucks me with that thick finger, pretending it's his swollen cock. Wanting him deeper, I rock in time with the assault. Sparks of pleasure burst inside my channel, igniting the insatiable hunger that exists in the depraved part of my soul. Rubbing my nose along his neck, he growls his own satisfaction as I reach for his belt buckle and undo it. Then, everything moves in slow motion. The pop of his button, as I clench around that perfect digit moaning like a wanton slut. How his zipper catches, refusing to budge. His grunt in frustration for it taking too long. Mine that matches.

"I want you to come," he husks as I force his zipper down. If I break the damn thing, who cares. I can buy him a new pair of jeans.

"Not until you're in me," I pant, resting my forehead on his shoulder. Mouth slack, I draw in shallow, needy breaths and scoot backward on his thighs to snake my hand inside his jeans and extract his member. Big releases the softest moan as I wrap my fist around the thickness, delighting in the pulse that thrums against my overheated skin. Pre-cum bubbles at the tip. I smooth the silkiness around the head with the pad of my thumb. So fucking sexy. If only I could suck it into my mouth and tease the V underneath with the flick of my tongue until he begs me to engulf him whole... to put him out of his misery.

Maybe later.

Big shudders, groaning as if my touch pains him in the best way. I jack him a few times for good measure, watching in fascination as another pearl of liquid pools at the tip.

Quickly removing his digit from my wetness, he grips my hips and forces me to my feet. I lose balance for half a second. Big's right there to keep me from falling.

"Hurry and take off your pants, Sugar Tits," he commands before tearing his own jeans and boxers down his legs to give himself more room to move. They pool at his ankles, above his well-worn motorcycle boots. I watch that veiny cock bob in the open air and slap his tattooed stomach as he swiftly removes his cut and shirt so we can be skin-on-skin, just the way we like it. I discard my bottoms, underwear, top, and bra in record time and kick them elsewhere to clean up later. Not wasting another second, I jump back onto his lap in my striped socks like it's Christmas morning, spread my limber thighs, and slam my pussy down on that dick. Air bursts from my lungs as he's buried to the hilt, stretching my walls to the max. Big's mouth drops open in a guttural cry as he palms my ass cheeks to fuck me on his shaft like I'm nothing more than a ragdoll he wishes to extract pleasure from. And I let him. Every part of me willingly falls victim to his expert onslaught. There's nothing better in the world than having a man own your body, doing what he does best to make you scream his name. So, I do. Embracing ecstasy beyond my wildest imagination.

Wrapping my arms around his neck, my swollen, milk-filled breasts smash to his pecs, and I give in. Up and down Big slams me onto his cock only to lift me slowly off and repeat the process over and over again. Moans of pleasure turn into incoherent mumbles. My nails bite into the nape of his neck on their own accord. Milk leaks from my tits, making a mess between us as they graze his chest. I nip at his collarbone when he hits my G-spot with the most exquisite thrust.

"Big," I beg, needing him, needing just a little more. I'm almost there.

He kisses the side of my head, lips pressing into my hair, warm breath bathing my scalp, somehow making me hotter for him. "I've got you. Come on my cock, baby."

And I do. As if he lit the fuse with a single, profound command, I fall. Soaring higher and higher until I explode into a billion fragments of never-ending bliss, eyes squeezing shut, chest heaving to catch my next breath. Sweat and breastmilk slickens our skin as I wail his name, tap-dancing the line of reality and a dream world where nothing but happiness and the love of my life exists.

My arms go slack, the orgasm draining everything from me. Turning me into a pile of boneless mush.

"That's it, babe. I love you so fuckin' much." Another kiss is deposited onto my sweaty hair as the onslaught continues.

"And I... I love... you," I breathe, feeling my heart swell with endless admiration and love deeper than anyone could've ever felt in the history of the world.

Big's movements slow and he wraps those sexy arms around me. I cling to his strong and steady warmth, never wanting to let go. The sudden burn in my nose is a surprise as are the tears that well behind my eyelids. I swallow thickly, refusing to let this intense... whatever, override my system completely, thus turning me into a blubbering hormonal mess. Not today. Not now.

I nuzzle my nose to the top of his pec, to keep the emotions at bay.

Tracing fingertips up my spine, Big slips those wandering digits into the base of my blonde locks, where he takes a firm grip and draws my head back. No sooner is my head pried from his body, do his lips cover mine in the sweetest most sensual kiss. Then I feel it. The release. Big groans, delving his slick tongue inside my mouth the moment he fills me with cum. His hips jerk in shallow thrusts, body trembling slightly as he finishes, drawing our session to a seamless close.

"I can't believe you're mine," Big mutters to my lips, his chest working overtime to catch his breath. A parting kiss is delivered before he rests my head against his shoulder to comb fingers through my hair.

"I am."

"Always."

"Yes. Always."

"Damn. It feels good to be inside you." Big flexes his still hard cock, buried deep. I squeeze around the thickness in return. You don't always need multiple orgasms to feel warm and fuzzy. This is nice, too. Perfection.

I kiss his shoulder. "I love it."

Big pats my bare bottom affectionately. "You can do whatever ya want for Christmas as long as it isn't overkill."

"I know. Thank you."

"Anything for you, Sugar Tits. Anything for you."

Oh, how I love this crazy, amazing man.

TWO

Wednesday, December 10, 2014

"Shh. Shh. Shh. Harley, please stop crying for Mommy," I beg at the end of my rope, tears teeming down my cheeks, eyes puffy from the never-ending emotional upheaval.

Cradling my daughter in my arms, I rock her, using a hand to pat her back as she shrieks her hatred for me, squirming against my bare chest. We're in her bedroom upstairs. I'm sitting on the pink glider, doing my best to get this situation under control. But she won't stop crying. Won't stop screaming bloody murder. Her face is beet red, snot coating both her and my shoulder as she smears her nose against me. Everything was fine this morning. Big left to work at the clubhouse and do what he always does. I fed her, changed her, and she played with her toys. Then came her afternoon nap, which went off without a hitch. During her downtime, I cleaned what I could before she woke up. The laundry is still in the washer, dishes need put away, and the kitchen is a disaster of epic proportions. I baked cookies like I do. Two dozen for mid-holiday season snacking. I even added the green and red chocolate chip mix for a festive flair. The next thing I knew she woke up wailing and I forgot to listen for the timer. I fucking missed it! The fire alarm sounded before I realized what was happening. Who does that? I haven't burnt cookies since I was a teenager. And you can bet your sweet ass they're charred—black as coal. The acrid smell is terrible as it lingers in the house. I haven't even had time to scrape the skeletal remains off the cookie sheets because my daughter is losing her shit.

The worst part is... I dunno what to do. This has never happened before. Not like this. Harley's been inconsolable for what feels like hours upon endless hours. I fed her at my breast and even that was a battle. She bit a nipple in retribution and she still hasn't chilled out. I changed her diaper, gave her a bath, rocked her, hugged her, and sang, among fifty other worthless things. Nothing has worked. I thought maybe she had gas, so I listened to her tummy and pumped her legs. Everything seems normal, apart from the wailing. There's no fever. I used a cold washcloth on her gums in case she was teething. She hates pacifiers, so they are of no use. Music hasn't even calmed her the slightest. This is awful. On top of being a failure at calming my kid down, I can't keep the house up, or write.

My first book published last month. It did okay. Better than I expected. Working from home is a dream come true, especially since I don't have to change out of my pajamas to work. To be honest, I thought it would be easy. That I'd write, publish, and be the perfect partner and mom in the process. But I'm not. It's all wrong. My list for today has been ruined, and it's my fault. I didn't plan for this. The icing on the cake is that Christmas is three weeks away and I have no clue what to buy Big. Today was the day I was gonna hunker down to find the best present ever; so he'd fall in love with Christmas like the Grinch did when his heart grew three sizes. That's when he'd embrace the holidays year after year, and they'd stop being an uphill battle. But I haven't had a moment to do that either. And you best forget about me calling someone. I don't need help. I've got this. Even if Pretzel doesn't think so, as he gazes up at me from the floor with that you're-a-failure look in his mismatched eyes. At least his doggy Christmas sweater offsets the judgy expression that makes me feel like the worst person in the world. We can get through this. I'm a mom. Moms are supposed to tackle everything and be a badass doing it. I refuse to pawn my daughter off on someone else, not like mine did when I was a child. Harley has to fall asleep eventually, as do I. I'm exhausted to the depths of my marrow. Our matching meltdowns aren't helping, I know. But I'm trying. Cut me some slack, okay? Not everyone is perfect. I sure as hell ain't. Parenting is hard as fuck.

Swapping my baby to the other shoulder, I continue to rock her. Harley kicks me in the stomach, her sharp fingernails scratching at my bare flesh, leaving marks. "Shh. Shh. It's gonna be alright. We're gonna be okay," I hiccup, wanting to believe the bullshit I'm spewing. At one point I tried laying her in her crib to cry it out. That lasted all of five minutes before a giant boulder of guilt steamrolled right over me, forcing me to give in, or die a thousand maternal deaths.

Inhaling deep, through my nose, my lungs inflate to full capacity before I hold the oxygen and slowly release it out into the atmosphere. With it, I hope to expel some of this awfulness boiling inside. It does no good. I still feel like hell.

Pretzel groans from the floor, rolling onto his side, unimpressed with my poor parenting skills. That makes two of us.

Harley lifts her wobbly head and uses it as a

weapon to whack into the side of my face. Which only serves to make her scream louder upon impact and my jaw to ache. A fresh batch of overwhelmed tears make their descent. My hands are too occupied to clear the wetness. Fat droplets of shame trail to the tip of my chin where they huddle together before swan diving downward, landing on my chest. They don't stop there. Some soak in, other's follow the valley to my stretch marked post-baby belly. That's where they find grooves to make their home.

"Bink?!" Big's voice booms loud and angrily above the wail of our daughter. Half a second later he shoves her bedroom door open and swallows up the entire frame as he steps across the threshold, entering the war zone. A flash of annoyance morphs his features and is quickly replaced with concern. Ugh, not that look. I don't want his pity. I've got this.

"What's goin' on, babe?" His tone's sickeningly calm, almost sweet.

I look away, staring at the crib, blinking away tears that skew my vision. "Nothing." I'm resolute, even if I'm quivering inside, desperate for this to end. He needs to leave. I didn't need Big's help before, and I don't want it now.

I sense him moving deeper into the space,

hovering close but not close enough that I'll lash out. Sometimes I wish he didn't know me so well. "Why are you and Leech havin' a meltdown?"

"S-she hates me." After today, I'm convinced it's true. More liquid hurt trickles as my daughter grips a piece of my hair and yanks hard. I let her. She's mad at me. It's fine. I don't mind. It's my fault she's upset. I deserve it.

Biting my bottom lip, I suppress a wince.

"Baby, she doesn't hate you. How long has she been like this?"

That's easy for him to say.

"Hours," I blubber.

"Christ. Why didn't you call?"

Because I don't need help.

Straightening my spine, I twist my head to garner unfailing eye contact, so he knows I'm not weak. "I'm her mom."

Big smirks as if he's about to call my bluff. "So? I'm her dad."

"I've got it handled." It doesn't matter that there's blood on my chest from her lashing out, or hair missing. I've been through worse.

"Doesn't seem like ya do. Give her to me, Sugar Tits." Big reaches out to take Harley as his intense blues land on my exposed breasts with interest. "Why you half naked?" A pair of mischievous brows bounce.

Not giving her up, I hug my arms around Harley's squirmy body. "I tried to feed her, but she didn't eat much."

"Can you blame her? Who wants to suck someone's titties who's been cryin'?"

What a jerk.

"Fuck. Off," I snarl, still crying despite my outrage. "I've got this."

"No. Ya don't. Now give me our daughter and go take a shower. You're a mess."

"I'm fine."

"No. You're not. You're bein' a stubborn ass. Parenting isn't easy. It's also not a one person job. I've told you to call me if you need me."

"I don't need you."

Reading my foul, brokenhearted mood like the Bink expert he is, Big shoves the ottoman to the side, and kneels in front of the glider, abs brushing against my shins. He doesn't try to steal our daughter away. Big massages the tops of my thighs instead, imbuing them with his steady warmth.

I kinda hate him for knowing me so well. But I'm thankful for his touch.

Those concerned baby blues crinkle around the edges and catch mine in their mighty web. "I love you, and I love our girl, babe. You had moments like this when you were a baby, too. Where you cried for no reason. Let me take that burden. You're upset, and that's only serving to make her more so. She feels you, sweetheart. You're tense and agitated. But you're also hurting. Give me our daughter, Bink. You know she's safe with me."

I know she is. That's what makes this so hard.

"But I'm a failure," I admit. "I wanna fix this." *Please let me.*

"You're not, babe, you're not. Let me fix this for *her*."

Finally hearing her daddy's gentle albeit deep, sensual voice through her sobs, Harley quits lashing out and twists half her body around. Wanting her daddy, she thrusts her chubby arms out at him. Big doesn't hesitate to reach underneath her armpits and draw her body to his much larger one. I let her go, having no other choice.

Cradling her in his massive arm, cocooned against his chest, Big rocks her there, whispering sweet nothings that don't fix everything, but calm it exponentially. Tension bleeds from my muscles as Big climbs back onto his feet, wiping the tears from her reddened eyes with his thumb. He gazes down upon Harley like she's his sun and moon, and kisses her forehead. A heartbeat passes before Big lifts those lovestruck eyes and looks straight at me as if I'm the universe in which he revolves.

"I've got this, my love. When you're done cleaning up, we'll be in the livin' room waiting for you. Take your time." Big delivers an easy, heart-melting smile before departing with our daughter in his safe embrace. Pretzel, not one to be without Harley for any length of time, follows them out.

What a mess.

I slump in the glider, combing fingers through my disheveled hair, legs stretched out in front of me. Milk leaks from my engorged breasts, joining the tears that have dampened my stomach. I've gotta pump soon. Should've done it this morning when Big left. Just add that to my ever-growing list of daily failures.

Big's right, though, I need to shower. No use in fighting it now that he's home. Part of me appreciates the intervention, while the larger chunk feels... worthless. But I can't fix that either. What's done is done. He's got Harley, and I'm not gonna accomplish anything by sitting here sulking. You can't always win.

Forcing myself to move, I use the chair arms to heft my tired form from the seat, and pad out of Harley's bedroom to ours. Where I flip on the shower in the adjoining bath to acclimate the temperature and strip off my pajama bottoms and underwear. The mirror above the sink fogs as I climb under the scalding heat of our rainfall showerhead. This is just what I needed—a silent moment to unwind. Water sluices down my curves as I scrub the day's sorrows away with my loofa. I wash my hair and the remaining tension sloughs off, swirling down the drain alongside the suds.

Maybe it's times like these that I need to stop being such a stubborn mule and ask for help. Big is Harley's father. He loves her and me. Why do I keep biting off more than I can chew? Being a mom is already hard enough. Infants aren't easy. Ones that are starting to crawl and teethe are worse. Now that I opened a Facebook clubhouse for my readers and I'm writing the second book to my series, I'm stretching myself thinner and thinner. Organizing a Sacred Sinners Christmas is a full-time job in itself. Last week, the Sacred Sisters and Deke helped set up a real tree in the clubhouse common room. Their kids decorated it with homemade ornaments as Mickey,

Gypsy, and Gunz built the larger-than-life Santa throne to sit beside it. It's fit for a king and perfect for Santa Claus or our biker version of the jolly fella.

I finish my shower and dry off with an extra-fluffy towel from the rack. Wrapping it around my chest, I amble into our adjacent walk-in closet and steal one of Big's Harley Davidson t-shirts off a hanger. Plucking a hideous nursing bra from the floor, I wrangle it on these too large breasts before shoving Big's top over my head and snatching a pair of Nickelodeon pajama bottoms out of the built-in drawer on my side. They're men's, but way too small for Big to steal. Not that he would. They're covered in '90s cartoon characters like The Rugrats and Ahhh!! Real Monsters. Having grown up during that decade, I'm impartial to them. They sure beat the crap on TV nowadays. Don't you agree? Although, I must admit I love the return of My Little Pony. That was another show I worshiped growing up, along with Care Bears, Gummy Bears, Eureka's Castle, Fraggle Rock, and The Smurfs.

Aww... the good ole days.

Oh... and don't let me forget Pee-wee Herman, ALF, and Transformers. My brothers and I used to fight about who the best Transformer was. Anyone who says anything besides Optimus Prime has lost their damn mind. Brew still believes Bumble Bee is where it's at.

Puh-lease.

I bought him an Optimus t-shirt for Christmas this year. Shhhh, don't tell him. It's a surprise. Figured since he won't wear it his wife can. Or Jizz can steal it. He likes them all.

To keep my feet from freezing, I slide on my unicorn slippers that are lined up next to our unmade bed. It's snowing outside. We got three inches last night. Gunz used the compound's mower with plow attachment to shovel the snow away. It gets piled where the kids' jungle gym sits. There's plenty of room for it to collect there. The kids love it too, because when it gets high enough they can sled down the mounds. Okay, let's be honest, it's not just for the kids. The men embrace their inner child and often join in. That's what makes living on the compound so much fun. We're surrounded by family at all times.

I know... I know... I'm stalling... blathering on. Am I at least keeping you entertained? The last thing I wanna do is face Big after what he walked in on. Figures, all it took was five minutes with her dad and Harley's through screaming. Mom doesn't have the magical healing powers. I'm a milk cow, nothing more. He's the fun one. *Argh.* I gotta stop this or I'm gonna end up bawling again. It's not Big's fault she likes him better than me. In my experience, dads are better than moms anyhow. Mine was shitty. Good riddance, as far as I'm concerned.

Stalling further, I re-enter the bathroom to brush my damp hair and my teeth. So I won't stink, I liberally apply deodorant, spritz on body spray, slather myself in a layer of body butter and insert disposable pads into my bra to catch any leakage. When all that's done I step in front of the mirror and give myself a once over. There's not much to see. Straight blonde hair that almost touches my shoulders. Blue eyes that look like they haven't seen an ounce of sleep in ten days. They're still puffy from Cryfest 2014. I'm not ready to face the music, yet. There's too much to be done that I have no damn energy to do. Adulting can kiss my fat butt.

Continuing to stall, I sit on the closed toilet lid, remove my slippers, and prop my heel on the edge to paint my toes ruby red with a silver glitter top coat for Christmas. If Harley liked me, I'd paint her toes, too. But she doesn't. At least not today. Perhaps I'll luck out tomorrow. I know I sound like a big baby right now. There's no excuse for it. Today just hasn't been the greatest, as you can tell.

"Bink!" Big hollers somewhere outside the bedroom, probably the hallway. Wouldn't it be easier if he came to talk to me face to face? Le sigh. *Men.*

Unable to move until my toes dry, I return his holler with one of my own. "What?!"

"Get your fine ass out here!"

"I'm busy!"

"Yeah, sulking!"

This is what happens when you fall in love with the same asshole who helped raise you, he knows every quirk, every pitfall of your existence down to your silliest ones. So what if I don't want my nose rubbed in the fact that my daughter is happiest when she's not in my arms, or when I'm rocking her or loving on her. Don't all mothers obsess over this? I dunno, but it doesn't make my pathetic issue any less real.

Big's not one to be ignored. "Bink!"

Sheesh... "What?!" Leave me the hell alone.

"We love you!"

Great. Hit me right where it counts, Big. Hit me where it fucking counts. This is so unfair. Can't even sulk for an hour without his interference.

We love you.

I know. Okay. I know. I fricken *know*!

"I'll be out in a minute!" I concede, shoulders slumping as I blow on my toes to dry them faster.

"You've got two or I'm comin' in after ya!"

Of course you are, control freak.

I count to thirty in my head—the Mississippi way. Then stuff my feet back into the slippers. If the polish gets ruined, we know who to blame... the old man. I tidy up the bathroom before heading their way.

In the hall, I stop short of entering the main quarters, to behold the craziest, most heartwarming display in existence ever to happen. Silly tears sting my eyes at the sight, as emotions clog my throat. Big has just finished cleaning the kitchen, and there's a stack of sorted laundry on top of our long, ten-person walnut table. There's a pizza box resting on the granite island from my second favorite pizza place. The first being Dewey's in Kentucky, which is too damn far to travel for pizza in the winter. The scent of hot, bubbly cheese and dough overpowers the burnt cookie stench. In the living room, Harley's asleep in a pair of pink footed jammies, lying on the floor next to the lit Christmas tree, legs and arms sprawled out in the cutest way imaginable. Pretzel's head is resting on her belly. It rises and falls with Harley's even breaths. I can't see his eyes, but I imagine he's asleep as well.

"Babe." Big addresses me from behind the island as he pulls paper plates from the cupboard closest to our six-burner stovetop. Shirtless, clad in a pair of black, low-slung knit pants in extra-long, his muscles ripple between movements as he lays the plates beside the box. With them, he sets a roll of paper towels and a half-empty bottle of ranch, my go-to pizza topper.

I pad to the opposite side of the island and flip open the pizza lid. Big reaches into the box before I get a chance and fishes out three pieces. Then he drizzles ranch across the top of them and hands me the plate with a paper towel strip tucked underneath.

"Go eat." Big tilts his head toward the living room, where we sometimes spend mealtime together.

You don't have to tell me twice.

"Thanks," I mutter.

My stomach audibly growls her hunger. I haven't eaten a thing all day. Saliva pools in my mouth at the mere thought of food. Pizza's perfect.

Heeding Big's order like a good baby mama, I do as I'm told and sit on the same black sofa we screwed on recently. I rest the plate on the puffy arm and the napkin in my lap as I curl my legs under. Big joins me a minute later, carrying his plate and two bottles of water. He tosses one into my lap, then finds his own spot on the couch.

Together, we eat in companionable silence with only the sound of Pretzel's high-pitched snores and Harley's sleepy coos to serenade us.

Three slices polished off, I wipe my mouth and fingers with the paper towel and gulp half the water bottle down. "That was great," I praise. Big deserves it. He pulled through even though I didn't ask for help, nor want it. If he hadn't interfered, I'd be fixing dinner right now. Not relaxing on the couch in pajamas beside my sexy, half-naked man.

I set my trash on the floor to redd up later. Big follows suit, then slaps the tops of his thighs. "Take off those slippers and put your feet up here."

I do what he asks knowing what's to come. "You're spoiling me tonight," I comment, stretching into his lap, wiggling my toes, nails polished to perfection. Guess they were dry when I slid those slippers back on after all. There's not a single ding in the gloss.

Big cuffs his mitt over my foot and presses his thumb into the arch, digging in just right. It feels damn good as I sprawl out on the sofa, using the arm as a pillow to prop my head on.

"You had a rough as fuck day. Didn't even have time to work, did ya?" he asks, massaging each toe

53

one by one.

Tucking my arms beneath my breasts to get comfortable, I bite back a satisfied groan. "No."

"Did you put ointment on those cuts ya got from Leech?"

I give him a lazy side-to-side head shake. "Nope."

"You need to do that."

"Yessss, dad," I drone, curving a partial smirk, eyes drooping to half-mast. If he keeps this up, I'm liable to fall asleep right here.

Big snorts his amusement. "Fine. Don't. See if I care when they get infected."

Smartass.

He would care. A lot. Then give me hell about it for a week, 'cause that's how we roll.

"They're not gonna get infected," I reassure in a playful mocking tone, nudging his abs with my toes to pick on him.

He pokes my calf in payback. "If you say so."

"I do." Time for a subject change. "How's the club?"

Big switches to my left foot. A raging boner prods my right as it resettles on his lap. He pretends the stiffy doesn't exist. I do the same. "Same old, same old. Gunz said his brother is comin' for Christmas."

"I know. He told me last week. Is he bringing

MC CHRONICLES: VOL 5

anybody with him?" Bonez is Gunz's brother. They're close in age, share similar looks. He's in the Corrupt Chaos Motorcycle Club which serves as a support club to us when necessary. Their brotherly relationship has dwindled on and off over the years. This'll be the first he's spent Christmas with us in God knows how long. It's nice to see their bond rekindling after a rough drought that neither of them will cop to. Trust me, I've asked.

"Not that I heard," Big replies.

My bottom lip juts into an exaggerated pout. "No Whisky then, huh?" She's the Corrupt Chaos's leading old lady. Basically, she's their me. Except she's older, owns a badass bakery, has wild red hair, and older kids. Her old man, Sniper, is their prez.

Big reaches out and plucks my bottom lip with his thumb and forefinger, single dimple grinning like I'm the cutest thing he's ever laid eyes on. Those baby blues alight with love. "No, babe. No Whisky. Not this time. Speakin' of Sacred Sister shit, when are you havin' that wrapping party?"

"The Saturday before Christmas. Debbie already has an itinerary for you guys to follow." Not that they'll follow it. Men... biker men to be more specific, don't like taking direction from the female persuasion if it's cut and dry, laid out for them. If we do it subtly, then it's all fine. Because they don't pick up on it. God forbid we assert ourselves.

See.

Case and point.

Big's scrunched-up expression is a prime example of the male biker resistance. "Are you serious? Does she think we can't handle a bunch of kids by ourselves for one evening?" His nostrils flare their indignation.

I refrain from rolling my eyes. Don't want him to stop massaging my feet, which is oh-so-amazing.

"No. She doesn't. Neither do the rest of us," I admit, knowing this'll push all the wrong buttons.

Twisting his head my way, Big glares at me. The valleys in his forehead deepen, brows knitting together as he pauses the massage to clamp his mitt around my foot. It's not enough to hurt. The cords in his neck tighten like thick banjo strings. "What the fuck?"

"Do you really think Bulk can handle both of his kids without Jez? How about Brew with little Dylan?" They can't.

"That don't mean I need fuckin' notes on how to care for my kid." Never said he did. He's a good daddy. But that doesn't mean his brothers aren't clueless motherfuckers when it comes to child-rearing. Dixie has her hands full with Brew and son.

I nudge his thigh with my heel. "It's not about you, Big. It's to keep the kids occupied. She's got games, snacks, and stuff all planned."

"Fine." He relents on a grumbled sigh and resumes the massage by pushing up my pant legs to work on my ankles. "You gonna be cool if I sleep at the clubhouse with Leech that night, so I don't have to wake her up to bring her home when y'all are done?"

"If that's what you wanna do. But... you're giving up the opportunity to fuck me when I'm drunk." One of his favorite pastimes. Not that it's happened a whole lot. But it has happened. Drunk sex is fun sex. Nod if you agree. You're nodding, aren't ya?

"We'll be home," Big rushes out, recognizing his error.

"Thought so," I snicker. God, I love this man.

"Maybe you'll let me put it in your ass." Those animated eyebrows bounce suggestively.

Not in this lifetime. Maybe if his pecker was smaller.

"Keep dreaming, bucko. It's never gonna happen. Not even when I'm drunk. A finger is all you're gonna get."

"Fuck." Big throws his head back, eyes slamming shut. "I'm hard just thinkin' about it."

I brush my foot against his velvet steel for emphasis. "You were hard before that."

"True. But my boxers are wet now. We gotta stop talkin' about sex before I flip you over, yank down those cute as hell pajama pants and fuck you facedown on this couch."

I open my mouth to protest that idea before he asserts his dominance and follows through. It wouldn't be the first time.

Big beats me to the punch. "I know you're tired, babe. I'm just sayin'..."

"You're a horndog, I know what I signed up for." A lifetime of daily fuckery. When ED comes a-callin' he'll be popping the tiny blue pill like it's Pez.

"Is that your way of sayin' I can fuck your sweet pussy on this couch tonight?" Big tickles my clit through my bottoms with his thumb. It sparks a little something there. Something I'm too tired to acknowledge.

Full belly laughing at his insistence, I shove his giant mitt away. "Stop. That's not what I said."

"I think it is. Just say the words, '*Big, fuck my sweet pussy. I'm wet for you. I want your big dick inside me.'*" Big tries and fails to mimic my girlish lilt as he flips his hair like a damn diva.

My laughter persists, making my cheeks hurt from smiling too wide. "I don't talk like that."

Big nods, contradicting me. "In my fantasies you do. I jerked off at the clubhouse today thinkin' about it."

Lordy.

"At work? Jesus Christ, Big, we had sex at like midnight last night." It was hottttt, too. Sixty-nine, then doggy style, finishing with reverse cowgirl that had him blowing so hard he convulsed like an inmate getting the electric chair.

"I know. The more we fuck, the more I want it. It's a drug. Addictive as hell."

Shaking my head, I chuckle at his odd way with words. "My pussy's a drug. Good to know."

Big scrubs a palm down his face, groaning. "Fuck. Don't talk about your pussy, babe. No more. I'm gonna get blue balls. And I hate that shit."

"You masturbated at work, Big. You could do it again. Your hand works just fine." How much do you wanna bet he did it inside his office without the door locked?

"Why's Pretzel wearin' an ugly-ass doggy

sweater?" he asks out of nowhere.

A tiny smirk. "Nice subject change."

"Glad you approve." Big's chest puffs in sarcastic pride.

"I thought it was cute. That's why he's wearing it." Why else would I have bought it?

Lips pressed together, glancing this way, Big delivers an unimpressed stare down. "He's a Pit, Sugar Tits," he states, then pauses as if he wants that small fact to sink in. I know what my pup is. Don't need him to clarify.

When a sufficient amount of time lapses Big carries on. "He's not a fuckin' Yorkie, Cockapoo, dumbshit whatchamacallit dog. Those are the dogs who wear ugly-ass sweaters. Not Pitties."

"Mine does," I state matter-of-factly, brooking no room for argument. Hating on Pretzel's sweater because of his breed is like saying Big shouldn't wear sexy lounge pants designed for twenty-somethings. The point is, he can rock out whatever he wants because he's Big. Just as Pretzel can sport a fancy, needlepoint doggy sweater if he wants. The clothes don't make the man. The man makes the man. If a thick-shouldered Rottie ran in here wearing a pink tutu, underneath it all he's still a Rottie. And yes, I know I said *he*. Boys can wear tutus, if boys wanna wear tutus. Own your shit. Case closed. Mic drop.

Now, where were we?

Yielding, Big drops his head against the back of the couch and looks up at the ceiling. "I'm not sure which is worse, the ugly sweater or the fact this massive hard-on is goin' to waste."

"You changed the subject, and we already agreed that your hand functions just fine to relieve your penile ailment. Plus, I can't have sex right now or I'll fall asleep. And I've gotta pump. My breasts hurt." I cup the mounds for emphasis. The pads inside my bra will be soaked through soon.

Big blindly traces his fingertips up my calves to my knees, where he proceeds to rub, inching closer to my center the more we discuss sex. "I can suck the milk out. No need to pump."

If I had a nickel for every time Big offered his milking assistance, I'd own a brand-new Harley, straight off the lot.

"How many times do we have to go over this? My breast milk is for Harley's consumption. Not Big's."

"I like the taste," he admits without an ounce of shame. Sometimes I wonder what the brothers would say if I told them about Big's breast milk fascination. Would they razz him? No. They'd probably give him a high five and ask for a sample. Which would turn ugly, real fast. They'd end up on his shit list with a black eye and the whole club would still know of Big's temporary fetish. Yet nobody would speak of it again, in fear of getting their ass handed to them.

"I know. You put it in your cereal twice in the last month."

So gross. How do I know this? I asked when two freshly pumped bottles disappeared.

"We were runnin' low on 1%."

Excuses. Excuses.

I sigh, snuggling deeper into the couch. "Right. So you used Harley's milk instead of going to the clubhouse to get some."

"It's sweet," Big explains, sliding his palm higher to *"massage"* my thigh.

To let him know I'm onto his pervy game, I slap the back of his hand but don't force him to remove it. The rubbing does feel good, as long as he stays on task. "You're one kinky fucking bastard, ya know that?" I tease.

Big winks, blowing me a flirty kiss. "Who's crazy in love with his woman, her pussy, ass, and tits that leak delicious milk."

Do you see what I have to live with?

That would be hella sweet if he weren't trying to

coerce me into bed. Okay, it's still sweetish... and a smidge cheesy, too.

"You can compliment me all day, we're still not having sex," I clarify to torment him. One way or another I'll have a dick in me before bedtime. When my man's on a mission, nothing gets in his way. Not even my exhaustion, or his.

"What if I put the rest of the laundry away and do the pumpin' for ya?" Big offers, nervous energy vibrating off him in potent waves. He really wants sex tonight. That doesn't surprise me, he's been hard this entire talk. Dirty thoughts are no doubt running rampant in that sex-starved brain of his.

"You gonna clean bottles out, too, and put our girl to bed?"

"I was already gonna do that anyhow," he remarks as if that was a silly question to begin with.

Now he's speaking my language. I dunno about you, but when my man does nice things for me, I wanna screw his brains out all the more.

"Can I be lazy in bed?"

Big grins a lascivious grin. One that speaks of naughty thoughts and even naughtier promises. "Is this your way of sayin' you wanna lay on your stomach while I fuck you, sweetheart?" He licks his bottom lip as if tasting me there.

"Yes," I breathe. "But I want your tongue before and after." Orgasms. Give them to me. More and more until I'm left a puddle of sated goo who can't remember her first name, let alone how to stand on two legs.

"Done." A definitive nod. "Now let me get your pump while you pull out those gorgeous tits." Big lifts my legs off him, stands partway, then carefully resets my legs on the couch.

"I love you, silly man," I mumble to Big's lips as he bends down to peck me on them.

"I love you so much more. Now get to strippin'." My old man snaps his fingers twice and points to my breasts.

"Yes, sir." I salute him, trying hard to subdue a grin that wishes to break through this poker-faced façade.

"Fuck. You're killin' me. Let's get this done, I got pussy to eat for dessert."

Yes, you do, sexy man. Yes. You. Do.

Am I the luckiest bitch in the world, or what?

Merry early Christmas to me. Hallelujah.

THREE

Saturday, December 20, 2014

Sitting on the floor in the living room of my house, legs spread eagle, hunched over, wearing a pair of red-and-green-striped leggings and a red, long-sleeve t-shirt that says *When I Think Of You I Touch My Elf* in white glitter, I cut another section of wrapping paper. The outfit is courtesy of Jez. We all got the same buttery-soft leggings in our respective sizes and a shirt she insisted we wear tonight. Jezebel's shirt says *Santa's Favorite Ho*. Pixie's, *Jolly AF*. Debbie's, *Let's Get Plowed* with a smiling snowman face. Candy Cane's, *It Ain't Gonna Lick Itself* with a candy cane, obviously. Dixie's, *I'm On The Naughty List*. Jo and Beth have also joined us tonight since they're family. So has Jade, one of Pixie's shop employees, who's awesome. Her teenage son hangs at the club garage working on cars and bikes a lot. Because she's a sweetheart, Jez also got them shirts and leggings, too. Jo's says *All I Want For Christmas is Deke's Dick*. Not all that original, but true. They've been dating since before Harley was born. It's getting pretty serious. Any day now he'll be giving her a Property of cut. Jez took it easy with Beth's top, not wanting her to feel uncomfortable. It says *Gangster Wrapper* with a present underneath. It's definitely the most PG of the bunch since Jade's reads *Jingle My Balls, They're On My Chest*. She's a busty gal, if ya didn't catch the sassy drift.

Beside me, sharing the space, is Jo to my left and Debbie to my right. For convenience, I've designated spots throughout the upstairs for the sisters to stack their presents when they're through wrapping so we don't mix them up. Not that we will. Those stuffed under my tree are for us to take up to the clubhouse for the kids' gift from Santa, aka Gunz, and our white elephant exchange.

"Are you seriously wrapping all of Big's gifts in Grinch paper?" Jez asks, prancing around the room on her tippy toes with a fancy, Dollar Store wine glass in hand. We're trying to be highfalutin up in this bitch. But our snooty-falooty glasses don't have wine. We're drinking extra-strong frozen margaritas from them. I know, margaritas from wine glasses—we're classy as fuck.

"Hell yes, I am." I fold over the edge of Big's present, taping it too much so it doesn't come apart. They're boxers with the Grinch on them. Can ya tell

I'm going with a theme this year? Jez made him a Grinch shirt for me as well. It's green and says *The Grinch Is My Spirit Animal.* If he doesn't wear it, I will. She also designed Harley an adorable onesie that mimics the theme nicely with *My Daddy's The Grinch* scrolled across the front. We find it hilarious. Big's either gonna be pissed or roll with the sarcasm. We win regardless.

"I tried to find wrapping paper with elves fucking, but every place I looked online was sold out already," Jez comments to the room, already three sheets to the wind. She hasn't wrapped a single gift all night. Why would she? She's been too busy watching her favorite gay porn Christmas scenes, that're playing with no sound on the living room flat screen. Yes, you heard me... Gay Christmas porn. All the men are dressed in various festive outfits. From reindeer and Santa, down to Frosty the yummy, gay Snowman who enjoys riding an orange vibrator that looks very much like a carrot. He's got a nice dick, too. Long, thick, and veiny. It reminds me of Big's, if my man was twenty years younger.

Beth gasps as if Jez's comment is the most outlandish thing she's heard all day. Debbie snickers beside me, and Jade raises her hand to high-five Jez on her fantastic choice of wrapping paper. I shake my head at the whole exchange with a giant smile spread across my face. When we decided to have a girls' night, I assumed we'd drink a little, talk about our men, listen to classic Christmas music, and wrap gifts. Nowhere in that equation was gay porn, matching outfits, or drinking margaritas from wine glasses. Enameled Christmas ones, no less. You know what? I wouldn't change it for the world. I'm buzzing pretty good. Everyone's having a jolly ole time. Beth is getting her share of worldly experience, and my real sister, Jo, gets to insert herself into the Sacred Sisters where she belongs.

Finished wrapping Big's boxers, I grab one of Harley's toys off the couch behind me to wrap next. The Grinch paper is shoved toward the massive pile that anyone can use. Climbing onto my knees, I crawl to the mountain of colorful paper and select a glittery cartoon print for my baby girl's presents before retaking my hunched position, legs out. One style for her. One style for her daddy. This way I don't need name tags.

Tucked safely at my side is my empty drink glass and a roll of clear Scotch tape. I made sure we each had our own shears, tape, and pens. There's nothing worse than throwing sharp objects around the room because we're a pair short.

Jez grabs the margarita pitcher from the kitchen island and makes her rounds, topping each sister off. As she does this, Debbie uses her phone to hook up Christmas tunes via Bluetooth on the wireless speaker. It's set low enough we don't have to yell to hear one another talk.

"Give me your cup." Jez gestures to my wine glass. I hand it over. In plops the fresh strawberry margarita until it's filled to the tippy top. Slush runs down the sides as Jez returns it to me, its rightful owner. Ever the lady, I lick off the icy mess without thinking twice. Then down half the tequila-flavored slush. The hint of lime, strawberry, and salt barely touches the palate. Jose is too busy doing his job, getting us drunk as fuck. None of that no name, store brand crap for us biker bitches. We go for the gold. Brew saw to that. Dixie brought two bottles and the mix. I supplied the blender that Big uses for his morning protein shake. He's been on this workout, high-protein kick for a while now. Got some of the brothers in on it, too. They each bought the same silly blenders, including one for the clubhouse kitchen. They're like women—always gotta own the same thing as their friends. #MakeMeGag

"What're you gettin' Deke and his kids?" This comes from Candy Cane who's seated on the floor beside Pix and her curvy friend, Jade. They've amassed a large pile of already wrapped presents behind them, catty-corner to the tree. Those chicks aren't messing around. I've barely touched my hill of gifts. All of us have gone way overboard, that much is clear. The rule was to buy presents for your immediate family, one for your kid for Santa to hand out at our party on Christmas Eve, and a white elephant gift. No other stipulations were set in place. Christmas can be costly, and if we bought for everyone we'd fork out a fortune. Which is what I did, unbeknownst to Big or our checking account. I've been stashing cash since June to pay for Christmas. This way he didn't notice the uptick in spending.

Jo adorns the top of her finished gift with a red bow. "I got him some clothes. Nothing fancy. And the girls a ton of Barbie stuff. They both wanted doctor dolls, which is what I bought. A brunette and a blonde, so they don't get them mixed up."

"That's what I got for my daughter, too," Jez interjects from the kitchen, where she sets down the empty pitcher. "I got Bulk a set of handcuffs and new saddlebags for his bike."

That sounds like her. Practical mixed with kinky

bedroom entertainment.

"Axel wanted cologne and a gift card," Pixie adds, also intoxicated. She rarely offers anything to a conversation without a dose of liquid courage.

Giving her equally tatted friend undivided attention, Jade combs her fingers through the thick strands of jet-black hair draped over her shoulder. "Is that what you got him?"

Pix gulps a mouthful of margarita, rosy cheeks bulging like a chipmunk. "The cologne, yes." She nods as she swallows the last bit and licks the remnants from her lips. "But I bought him some of that expensive protein powder they're all drinking. I kept the spending under a hundred."

Eyes rolling, I groan. "We all bought our men that crap didn't we?"

The roomful of bobbleheads confirms it.

"And a shaker bottle," Jez says, swaying her hips in the middle of the room, next to the mountain of wrapping paper with a fist curled around the stem of a wine goblet of pink scrumptiousness.

"I got these new weights," Candy Cane adds, her focus on whatever gift she's taping.

"A jar of local honey." From Debbie.

Jez freezes mid drink, rim still stuck on lips as her

face twists into a scowl. "Dammit. I didn't think of the honey."

I didn't either. I got the protein powder that costs half a benji. We already have enough weights, and if I see a new shaker bottle, I'm liable to toss it in the trash. Wanna guess how many we have? Six. Six fucking shaker bottles. Dishes are done daily. Why do we need six bottles with those stupid metal shaker ball things that are a pain in the ass to place in the dishwasher? Okay... I need to take a breather. This is getting me worked up.

Pixie's fire has been lit. The red glow of alcohol-infused cheeks serves as proof. She tosses a petite hand out, movements sharp and exaggerated when she speaks. "Why doesn't one of them make those damn protein bars in bulk and share 'em? Am I the only one with a glass pan in the fridge with those things inside, taking up the entire top rack?"

Story of my life.

"I started putting them in Tupperware since I don't have room for a pan in my fridge. Nor the patience for that shit. And who does that? Put a *pan* in the fridge? Do you think they all decided they wanted to drive us insane by buying the same fucking glass pan and making the same stupid protein bars with the same stupid expensive mix? Not that I'm complaining, their bodies are looking damn nice. And the stamina in the bedroom is off the charts," Debbie says, releasing a low whistle at the end.

Jez slaps her belly, drawing our attention. "Have you seen Viper's stomach lately?"

Yes! It's insane.

I.N.S.A.N.E.

Candy Cane catcalls in appreciation.

Debbie two-finger whistles, making my ears ring.

"Hell yes," Jo tosses out and takes a sip of her margarita. "Who knew ten-packs existed?" She flicks a piece of messy bun off her forehead where it's fallen into her eyes. Most of us are slumming it tonight. No makeup. No fancy dos. Even I have my hair half up in a messy hive that teenagers rock with their leggings and Ugg boots. Whereas I look like a washed-up housewife. My blonde locks are too fine and too short to do much with. The remnants of my hair that won't stay up does what it always does—almost swishes the top of my shoulders in all its stick-straight glory.

"I think it's a fifteen-pack," Pixie contends.

It could very well be. We're talking washboard abs on top of washboard abs. The skin is taut, and his belly button is a cute slit hidden among the tattoos. The girls have every reason to drool.

"There's no such thing. It's a ten at most," Dixie throws in.

Jez double taps the side of her nostril, grinning like a dirty bird who relishes the attention. "He added that nose ring, too."

I sigh. So hot.

Deb sighs. Even Beth sighs...

"Totally fucking hot," Jade pitches forth.

Jo rolls up the sleeves of her red shirt, exposing her tats, and lobs another finished present onto the couch behind us. She's on fire. "And what about Gunz and those pecs? Are Big and he working out together or what? Those shoulders and chests on them both be bangin'."

Gross. Why is she talking about either of them that way? Gunz's body... Yak!

My face screws into a mask of sour-faced horror. "I love you, Jo, but if you say another word about Gunz's body, I'm gonna puke." All over her damn lap. It's true, I have seen most parts of Gunz's body. But it doesn't mean I wanted to. Shit happens when you run around the clubhouse on a night when the club whores are cruising. Gunz never has and will never be shy about his exploits. Most of them aren't. That doesn't mean it's pleasant to witness. That skull tattoo above his cock is burned into my retinas for all time. There's not a scrubber in the world strong enough to cleanse that memory or the Solo cup doozy with Blimp. Need I say more?

"What? It's niiiccee," Jo emphasizes, winking at me with a devil-may-care grin before she bumps her shoulder against mine.

I flip her the bird, and she pretends to catch the damn thing like I blew her a kiss. What a bitch. She's lucky I adore her crazy ass.

"Suck saggy tits," I hiss good-naturedly. That earns me a smirky eye roll. Deke is gonna have his hands full with that one. Not that Big doesn't have his full with me.

"Bulk has lost twenty pounds," Jez blurts outta nowhere, staring at the naked threesome on the TV with her back to me. "I swear his dick has grown three inches."

Think we all knew that. She brags about it... a lot.

"Yeah! Get it, girl!" Jo fist-pumps the air, cheering Jezebel on as if she needs any encouragement. She doesn't. Maybe we need to cut her off.

Seated in front of the unlit fireplace, legs stretched out, Dixie changes the subject. "Is anyone getting Mickey, Gypsy, White Boy, Mal, Blimp, Runner, or Viper gifts for Christmas since they don't got people to buy for them? I'd say Gunz, too, but I'm sure you've got him covered. Right, Bink?"

Casually, I bob my head and set Harley's wrapped gift on the couch before I snatch another. It's a new outfit. I might've gone overboard with the clothes. "Oh yeah. Way covered. I also got the rest of the boys' gifts." It's not much. Some cookies and a few odds and ends. Nothing expensive.

Dixie's mouth drops open. "All of them?"

"All of 'em," I confirm with a simple nod and shrug.

I don't see what the big deal is.

Candy Cane gasps and looks up from the strip of camo paper she's cutting to fit a shaving kit for her old man, Tripper. "Christ. Did Big lose his shit when he found out? He was pissed enough about the decorations."

That he was. We dealt with that, though. Apart from him kicking Jez's Nativity scene down on a regular, he's been fairly normal. If you consider grumbling about the holidays and the snow to be normal. He's tired of being cooped up. Riding is vital to a biker. The ice outside isn't safe, so he hasn't gotten any road therapy in weeks. That's bound to make any Sacred Sinner a grumpy asshole. More so my old man, because he's ... old, and set in his ways.

If Harley wasn't alive, he would brave the ice and salt to get that much-needed therapy. But he hasn't. Not because I said no. That would go over like a lead balloon. Big isn't dumb, he knows how dangerous it is out there when the conditions are sketchy. I don't want to lose him any more than he wants to lose us. Death isn't an option. That giant asshole better live to be a hundred, or I'm gonna knife his nuts when we reunite in Heaven—if we both make it there.

"I didn't tell him," I explain.

"You didn't tell him you bought them all something?" Candy Cane asks.

A firm shake of the head. "No. Because they're gifts from Harley and me. Not from him." My tone spikes a few ear-piercing decibels.

Big's not one to appreciate false gratitude. If I were to put his name on them and someone thanked him, he'd be angry, not pleased. The Grinch is hard enough to handle. I don't need the added stress.

Jo twists her body around to look at me straight on, both legs curled to the side. Her nose crinkles, shoulders rigid. "Sister, you did *not* leave him off the gift tags." She's stunned by this—daresay a bit appalled. She shouldn't be. Apparently, Jo needs more one-on-one time with Big and me to understand our unique dynamic.

Not taking Jo's misplaced judgment well, I toss the scissors down and give my aching back a break by leaning against the sofa to unkink the coiled muscles. I'm not twenty anymore. Thirty-one must be the new forty-five, because this lower back pain when wrapping is no joke.

Arching my spine backward, I exhale in relief as the discomfort dissipates. Then inhale deeply and let it out before addressing the crowd, more specifically Jo, who's waiting on me to respond. We snag eye contact from the side. "I sure did. He didn't pick out the gifts. He didn't bake the cookies. He didn't want Christmas for Christ sake. Why would I give credit where there is none?" Ipso facto, he wouldn't want the recognition anyhow... *Duh.*

Candy Cane raises her glass in pseudo applause. "Fuck yeah. You're right. You're so right."

"Maybe we should all do that. Leave them off. See how they like it. It's not like we don't do all the work," Debbie suggests, taping up a blue snowflake-wrapped gift.

"Axel helps with ours." *Ouch.* Pix rubs salt in our invisible wounds.

"Lucky bitch." Jez gives the blue-haired fairy a middle-finger salute and half-ass bow that has her careening to the side and stumbling over heavy zigzagged steps that rattle the pictures on the walls before regaining her balance. Pixie sticks her tongue out. I snort-laugh at their drunken antics. Bulk would pay good money to see his old lady like this. Too bad filming is against Sacred Sister rules. What's said between us, stays between us.

Jo raises her glass in cheers. "I'll drink to that." The rest of the sisters follow suit and sip, happy smiles all around.

"Lazy fuckin' bikers," Dixie adds, snickering behind the rim of her cup.

"I'll drunk to that, too." Jez thrusts her margarita into the air with flourish. Slush flies toward the ceiling and down it falls, onto her hands with icy bits raining onto the floor. Party foul. She'd better clean that up.

I point to the mess, arching an eyebrow at the brown-haired former harlot.

"I got it," she mouths apologetically with surprised cartoon eyes and scurries to the kitchen for paper towels.

Jo keeps the conversation rolling full steam ahead, messy floor be damned. "Don't hate. We love them… most of the time."

"With their pants down or their mouths between our thighs!" Jez hollers from the kitchen. She is a damn hoot.

An innocent "*eep*" emits from a cherry-cheeked Beth who covers her face, eyes downcast, to hide the singe of awkwardness. It's cute how virginal the woman is. We need to pump more tequila into Beth, and she'll whistle a less finicky, lily-white tune.

Shifting my gaze to the side, I bark a laugh as Deb hoists her near empty glass over her head. "Cheers to that!" she cries then drains the rest of her margarita in a single swallow.

Sauntering back into the living room, there's a roll of paper towels tucked underneath Jez's arm. She swivels her hips to Jingle Bell Rock and straddles the mess she made, a sock-clad foot planted on either side. "How much you wanna bet they aren't following Debbie's instructions tonight?" she states, bending her thick curviness at the waist to sop up the bits of liquid between her feet. It's not such a good idea when said feet rock onto the balls and back to her heels, way back, trying hard to keep balance and doing a piss-poor job at it in her state of inebriation. Not at all worried about falling on her face, Jez bends at the knees, unable to reach everything without doing so; even with those short legs vacuum sealed in red and green stretch fabric.

"There's no way they did," Dixie remarks.

I second that sentiment with a double nod.

"I baked sugar cookies for them to frost and everything," Debbie explains.

Dixie digs into the oversized reusable tote she brought to extract another bare present and sets it on the ground between her thighs. "Bet they locked the kids in a bedroom with some Christmas movie on so they could drink and eat all those cookies."

"Maybe we should ask White Boy to check it out for us," Jade suggests, picking up her cell phone from the floor and resting it on her legs.

"Did he come tonight?" I ask. He's a full-fledged member now, as he should be. But it's papa biker night, not mandatory for those who don't have children. He's still a baby in my eyes, skating just above legal drinking age. Hanging with kids when you're that age isn't considered cool.

Jade plucks the stomach of her red shirt, to keep it from clinging to the paunchy parts, which most of us have. Apart from Debbie, Pix, and Candy Cane—the skinny sisters of the group. "My son's there, so yeah, he'll be there too. Pixie said that was cool. He was over at the shop all day with the guys." Jade scratches the top of her thigh like she's nervous and won't make eye contact.

"No. No." I wave off her obvious concern that she's not welcome. They both are. Full stop. To ease her wariness, I keep going with a sugary tone. "That's great. Send him a text. See what he says."

Candy Cane speaks up. "He'll be in a world of shit if any of the guys find out he's rattin' 'em out to the old ladies."

"They should know we've got spies everywhere," Jo defends, and she's not wrong.

"Gunz would tell me," I throw out. He would, too. Grandpa Gunz is the best grandpa any kid could hope for. Not that my dad isn't okay. He's here, sometimes. Harley's seen him and his old lady, Mandy, enough to know their faces. Aside from that, they're not the gushy grandparent type. He wasn't that way as a father either. I'll take what I can get. And don't even get me started on Jizz and Viper. Their uncle competition knows no bounds. Viper doesn't even care that Harley isn't biologically his niece. He loves her all the same, as do most of the brothers. Spoiled is the apt word when referring to Harley, or Leech, when you hear the men talk. Big has corrupted them all.

Jade types away on her phone as she talks. "White

Boy'll do it. His mama's my best friend and Blimp's sidepiece. If he doesn't tell us, I'll sic her on him."

"Who's his mama?" I ask, slicing through Harley's designated wrapping paper.

"Loretta."

Holy shit. I've never paid enough attention to notice that.

I look straight at Jade, eyes rounding to saucers. "Bartender, raspy-voiced Loretta? The one who's always blowing Blimp at parties in front of everyone?"

A crooked albeit amused grin. "That's her."

"She's your best friend?" I can't believe this. Loretta's been hanging around for years. Many, many, many years. Like since I was a child. Blimp has always been her chosen fuck buddy. Never understood why, because she doesn't smoke dope like he does. Though, I have seen her light a blunt now and again for him. She looks nothing like White Boy, apart from... hmm... maybe their bodies—they're both thin. This's insane.

Jade snickers. "By default, yes. She's my neighbor."

Makes sense, since Jade is nowhere close to Loretta's age.

"Oh, you must live on Cherry Street?" Evidently, I'm a nosy bitch tonight.

"Yup. Been there for goin' on seven years."

As Jade and I talk, Jo and Jez whip up another batch of margaritas while Pixie and Deb relocate their presents to their designated spot in the house to avoid mix-ups.

"Loretta's been a club whore for years. Why haven't I seen you around much?" I probe, genuinely curious.

An unapologetic shrug. "Bikers aren't my thing."

"Bikers aren't your thing?" Good for her. If I didn't grow up on the compound, they wouldn't be my thing either. Most of them are a bunch of alpha a-holes. Yet, I wouldn't change my past for a do-over. Big, despite all his pain-in-the-assness, I love the fucker.

"Nope. Too much trouble. I like my quiet life. No men. No hassles. Just me and my boy." Sounds like the story of a broken heart or damaged something or other. Can't say I've been there. I've only been in true love, whatever that means, once. Regardless of the baggage she carries, I hope she'll hang with us more. She fits in well, even without a Property of patch hanging on her back.

Before I get a chance to respond, Jade's face lights up with the biggest, most honest smile I've seen tonight while reading messages on her phone. She is practically giddy. A heartbeat later the smile vanishes and her features are schooled as if she's locking unwanted emotions down in their proverbial dungeon. "Josh... er... White Boy said Big set up a sleeping station in his bedroom. Most of the little ones are sleeping already. Viper volunteered to keep watch. The older kids and teens are playing pool and being *kids*... is what he said. I asked if they did the cookies and he said they did. That Gunz made everyone follow Debbie's protocol. Down to the lime punch with sherbet."

Debbie pads back into the living room and retakes her spot. "Remind me to kiss Gunz tomorrow for being a team player."

I bump my shoulder to hers. "Will do. I'm gonna give him one myself. It sounds like they're behaving."

Suddenly, Jade's hardened shell breaks into full-bore laughter. I press my lips together to prevent myself from joining in. But Candy Cane and Jo are goners. They follow right along with Jade for no reason at all. This goes on for some time until Jade blows out a breath to calm herself long enough to spit out whatever it is she needs to say. "Bink... umm... Big told Josh to," she pauses a beat to assuage another bout of laughter that threatens to reappear, "tell you to get your phone. He needs to know if you're drunk enough to come home yet."

Of course, he wants to know that.

Drunk sex.

Big left a lipstick note on our bathroom mirror expressing his elation for the inevitable sex. He'll be cleaning that red mess from the glass later. Bet he's been running around with a chub all night. If I text him now, he's gonna encourage me to kick the sisters out before we're done. It'll also turn me on because we all know his dirty mouth will be locked and loaded, much like his cock is ready to perform. The old man is insatiable.

"I'll get it later," I explain. "But don't tell him that."

Jade's full lips curve, lines forming around her eyes. "Think Big already knew you were gonna say that, because Josh just told me that Big expects to put the P in the V tonight."

My eyes roll so far I might get a headache. "He's quite the charmer."

Jade chuckles as does Pixie who leans in to confirm the silly texts.

If I don't respond in some form, he'll blow up everybody's phone tonight. Including mine, which I left in the bedroom. "Just say I'll let him play with his favorite toys later if he's a good boy." That should keep him happy for an hour or two.

"Bink!" Jez shouts from the kitchen, which is unnecessary, she's not that far away.

"Yeah?" I turn and watch her and Jo complete the finishing touches on our beverages.

Jez is reading from her iPhone. "Big just said to tell Sugar Tits that he'll tickle the kitty with his tongue tonight if she's a good wittle girl."

I grunt, nostrils flaring along with my irritation. "He did not text you that."

Jez hands Jo the fresh pitcher to refill our cups with and walks over. She tips her phone's face down enough that I can see her recent text from Big.

He did send that.

Jerk.

Another eye roll is warranted for this kind of outrageous behavior. I steal her phone, not needing her to fight my battles for me. Jez lets it go with a pleased smile. It should be embarrassing that everyone gets to hear how he talks to me, but it's not. Because it's not like they don't already know. He vocalizes crap like this in front of them with no remorse or consideration for decorum.

My thumbs get to work.

Me: *You'll lick this kitty all night long because you like it when I'm a very bad girl. Now leave us alone. The longer you bother us, the longer it's gonna take to finish.*

Big: *I want your pussy now. I don't care if you're good or bad. I've been hard for hours. Viper is watching our kid. Let's have a quickie in the basement. They don't gotta leave.*

Me: *Patience is a virtue, or haven't you heard?*

Big: *That sass does nothing to deter me wanting to bend you over the bed and go to pound town.*

Me: *Didn't think it would. Now go away, I'm busy with my sisters.*

Big: *They owe me.*

Me: *They don't owe you shit.*

Big: *I'm sharing you tonight. I don't share my woman.*

Sheesh. Sometimes he can be sweet in his own Neanderthal way.

Jo tops off my wine glass and sets it next to Debbie to keep it from spilling while I'm preoccupied.

Me: *Two hours. I'll be done by then.*

Big: *Fine. I'm walking in that door in exactly one hundred and twenty minutes. Expect two rounds. You'll be lucky if you can walk straight tomorrow.*

Promises. Promises.

Even though I don't want to, I grin, and just as I suspected would happen, my core clenches at his vow. There's something about that filthy mouth I enjoy way too much.

Me: *You'll survive. Love you. Peace.*

Big: *I love you way more, babe. Way fucking more. See you in two hours.*

Me: *Two hours.*

Finished, I slide Jez's phone back to her, retrieve my glass from Debbie, and gulp the first half of slush down. Time to wrap until my fingers wanna fall off and back is ready to shatter.

"Let's get this shit done. I've got orgasms waiting on me."

"Yeah, ya do!" Jez cheers from her spot on the floor, where she gets her drank and porn on simultaneously.

Another "*eep*" sound arises from a too sober Beth. Give that girl a pitcher all to herself.

Now, where's that Grinch paper, Big's socks aren't gonna wrap themselves.

FOUR

Christmas Eve
Wednesday, December 24, 2014

"Sugar Tits, it's time. Hand our daughter over to Deb." Staring off with the asshole who's got me cornered next to the jukebox, I glare way, way, way up at the mountain I call mine. His height is a pain at times like these, as is his sex appeal. I really should've picked an uglier partner.

I hug Harley closer to my breast, fingers combing through her fine, baby hair. She's asleep and has been for almost an hour. If I let her go, she might wake up. You don't want to wake a sleeping baby. It's not like there's any harm in me padding around the clubhouse in striped Christmas socks, holey skinny jeans, a low-cut red shirt, and Property of cut with *my* child curled against *my* chest like I'm the most important person in the galaxy. These times are far and few between when I'm competing with a cuddly Jez, Grandpa Gunz, and Big Dick Daddy-O, who, let's face it, has way more real estate to cuddle on than I do. Even though I got nice squishy boobs to use as pillows.

"No." I assert my position. Out of the corner of my eye stands a patient Debbie, waiting for me to screw my head on straight and hand over my first and only born. This isn't going to go over without a fight.

If my heart didn't physically ache every time I've tried to turn my kid over to anyone, I'd be fine. I'm not that irrational. And, no, I'm not drunk. I'm stone sober. It's just that it's my first Christmas Eve with her and we're bonding. Unless you're a mother, you could never understand that connection. The physical ache you feel inside your chest when you love someone so much that you can't bear to spend a moment away from them. And if you do, you feel like you might die. A tad dramatic? Yes. But it doesn't make it any less true. I just need a little longer. Another hour maybe. Two at most. Then I'll be ready to let her go. Today was too magical to break the spell quite yet.

Big bends to my height, steps too close and snags eye contact. "We. Agreed."

I take everything I said to him back. All of it.

If looks could kill, Big would have holes lasered through the center of his weirdly attractive pupils all the way through the back of his skull. "We didn't agree on shit," I lie.

Treating me like Pretzel when he doesn't obey, Big bops me on the tip of my nose. In turn, I try to bite that finger off with a vicious snarl. I'm slow, but he knows the intent, and that message is powerful enough. "Surrender our daughter to Debbie. Now. Babe. Please. She has already taken all the other kids back to Jez's for the night. It's past nine. No more children are allowed in the clubhouse. It's adult time."

"It's Christmas Eve." Best. Excuse. Ever. It's not like you can tell your man your heart hurts to let your baby go when she loves you today, giving you most of her smiles, smelling of candy canes and Grandpa Gunz—two of the greatest scents in the world.

The clubhouse party started at five. All the Sacred Sisters pitched in and brought dishes for a potluck of sorts. Mickey and Gypsy were also kind enough to contribute a meat and cheese platter. We didn't do fancy foods, we kept it simple: shredded chicken sandwiches, Ballreich chips, shrimp cocktail, a variety of salads, and more types of dessert than there are days in the month. We ate until our stomachs revolted, hung out, and did Santa with Gunz. Whose handy helper, Bonez, our designated elf, pulled the gifts from Santa's authentic sack to give to the *"nice"* kids.

"You planned this," Big reminds, giving me a you-are- crazy- as- fuck- but- I-love -you- so -it's- okay look.

Playing on Big's need to care for us, I reveal a portion of the truth. "I didn't know it'd be so hard to let her go. She likes me today. I want to document this forever."

I kiss the top of her soft, baby scalp. Harley nuzzles into the base of my throat, her tiny fists balled on either side of her head, one holding onto my shirt. A patch of drool has gathered on the bare skin where her mouth rests. She's the most adorable being ever created. The Mrs. Claus-inspired outfit emphasizes that adorableness to the millionth power. I can't wait to print copies of the pictures I took of her sitting with Gunz on the black Santa throne the brothers built. Next to the chair, kneeling to fit into the photo is the gray-haired Bonez. If you haven't met this man before, let's just say, you *want* to meet him. He's charismatic, sweet, considerate... and hotter than Billy Hell. If you're into mature gentlemen in their forties or older, as I am, then you'll love Bonez. He's thick, muscled, inked all over, and... did I mention the elf green, spandex leggings he's wearing today? They do nothing to hide the extra-long summer sausage he has stuffed down the inside of his well-defined thigh. Gunz bought the silly costume as a joke. Didn't think his brother would wear it. Much to the biker's dismay and the Sacred Sisters' luck, he's rocking that second skin like it was made for him. Including an elf hat with pointy ears and matching slippers where the toes curl. Those pecs should have sonnets written about them. They're *that* drool-worthy. Trust me, I'm not the only person who's noticed his yum factor. Jez has been shamelessly flirting with him all night. Bulk, the saint, is beyond amused with his old lady's pervy antics.

Big cups my cheek, trying a different tactic to ease our daughter from my hold without force. "We already documented it, babe, with the videos and millions of photos you and I both took with our phones today," he reasons.

"There wasn't a million," I argue to stall the inevitable. I hate when he makes sense. To be fair, it's not possible to have a million pictures of today. I'm not one of those "people." You know the ones I'm talking about, who post nothing but pictures and stories about their kids on social media as if they're the second coming. And don't even get me started on the people who do that with their dogs. I know that sounds harsh, but we all think it. I'm just ballsy enough to say it. I may go crazy with pictures, but I don't force feed them to anyone. They're for me to ingest. Not the *world*.

Still cupping my cheek with one hand, Big snaps his fingers in front of my face with the other. "Stop stalling. It's adult time. You've done mommy time and auntie time all day. Give her to Debbie."

Head shaking, I sigh loudly—a healthy combination of defeated and dramatic. "You don't get it."

"No, babe, I don't. I'm not her mom, I'm her dad. I don't get it. I'll never get it. I didn't carry our girl for nine months. I don't produce her food in my chest. I will never know the bond, babe. What I do know, is she's asleep. She'll stay asleep. You're not gonna miss another Christmas Eve moment with her. I promise. And if she wakes, we'll have Debbie text me, and I'll take you on over to Jez's to pick up our girl. We've got 'til midnight to have Bink and Big time together, with our family. In the morning we'll have more Leech, Mommy, and Daddy time. Stop making this harder than it has to be. Take a deep breath..."

Silly tears welling, nose stinging with the need to bawl my stupid hormonal eyes out, I inhale that lungful of air at Big's request.

"Now let it out."

I do, blowing it from my lips.

A hot tear trickles down the edge of my nose. Big brushes it away with the pad of his thumb and deposits the wetness on his pant leg. "I love you. I know how great today has been for us. Let's keep the great going... okay?" Jesus, I have the sweetest man sometimes. What did I do to deserve a life like this? I don't know. He's been great today. Not a single complaint about Christmasy stuff. He even loved helping Harley unwrap her pink light-up phone from Santa. I got that on film.

The mere thought of that precious memory has me wanting to lose it...

This has gotta stop.

I don't do crybaby crap.

Becoming a mom has made me soft.

A nod is all the answer Big gets unless he wants the waterworks to spring into action.

Reading the moment, Debbie steps forth with her arms out. Big pecks my pouty lips and our daughter's head before I pass her off. Another tear makes it descent. My lover catches that one too, as we watch Debbie carry our sleeping princess through the hall door to put her to bed.

Once she's gone, Big takes my hand into his much larger one and tugs me to the open space in front of the jukebox. He pushes a button on the thing, and a song I didn't know was on there blares to life. With no effort at all, he draws me into his warm cocoon, somehow knowing exactly what I need. *Him.*

Intertwining our fingers, Big presses the back of my hand to his pec as my arm curves around his side, palm splaying across an ass cheek. He wraps his opposite hand around the nape of my neck. My cheek presses to his sternum. Our feet slot together side by side like we've done this a zillion times before. Then, we slow dance. No words are spoken. The familiar scent of leather and Big— the love of my life—eases my fraying nerves. A content sigh slips free. My eyelids close as the rhythmic lub-lub of his heartbeat in one ear serenades me, while the classic Elvis hit, *Blue Christmas,* croons in the other.

Lost in the moment, of us, of him, of today, and how we got here... Years of memories claw their way to the surface...

We were in the clubhouse parking lot, it was a summer club party, and I was sitting on my bike without the key in the ignition, enjoying the sun beating down on my bare skin. Big leaned against

the brick of the clubhouse, a beer clutched in his mitt.
"Bink, you can't wear a fuckin' bikini top when
you're ridin' your hog. Your tits are gonna flop out.
Nobody needs to see a tit when they're ridin' down
the highway goin' sixty. You gear up, or you don't
ride. Always remember, prepare for the slide."

A sentimental grin curves at the recollection. Big
has always had his own brand of protectiveness when
it comes to me. Even when I was a teenager who
drove him and Gunz to the brink of insanity. That day
I had no intention of riding. I merely wanted to sit
and soak up the rays. I think he knew that, but chose
to tease me instead... To use that moment as a
teaching one, as he so often did.

I snicker as a different, yet somehow connected
memory surfaces...

It was one of the many days Big sat outside my
school building on his bike my second year of middle
school, waiting for me to be let out.
His face was stuffed in a book when I arrived.
"Whatcha readin', Big?"
He lowered said book and smiled his signature
way. Single dimple out in full force. A pair of dark
shades covered his eyes. There was a black bandana
wrapped around his forehead. "You're gonna be a

teenager next month."

I stood to the side of his Harley, ready to slide on when he said I could. "So?" I cocked a hip, hand perched on it. My loose blonde hair tickled the tops of my shoulders as a breeze blew through.

Big lifted the paperback so I could see the cover. It was a how-to guide on raising teenage girls. "You're already a handful. So Gunz and I are gonna read this. Don't wanna fuck shit up."

"You're not my dad, Big."

He shrugged like that didn't make any difference. "Yeah. Well. You're ours, and we take care of our own." His chin jutted toward the dip in my tank. I was one of those girls who developed early. Cleavage was unavoidable in most scoop-neck shirts. "No more clothes like that. I'll take you shopping."

"I'm not a nun."

"No. You're not a club whore either."

I gasped at his brashness that stung and made me wanna walk home, no matter the distance. What a jerk. Why didn't Gunz pick me up from school? Why did they ever send Big?

He never took me shopping, in case you were wondering. I avoided him after that, for as long as I could.

It's strange the things we remember and those we don't...

A kiss is pressed to the top of my head as Big guides our simple dance in a circle, careful not to step on my unprotected feet.

Lips linger in my hair, his hot breath bathing my scalp. I smile, it's soft and happy. A gentle warmth flitters its way through my veins, heating me from the inside out at our closeness. I nuzzle the side of my cheek to his chest, the cotton of his well-worn shirt is a creature comfort, lending way to yet another memory I've long forgotten.

Fingers combed through my blonde strands. The familiar drum of Big's heart against my ear as I laid my entire body on him, legs curled up. There were cartoons on the TV in the living room where we sprawled out on the couch. I coughed from the awful flu that wanted me dead.

Big patted my back to soothe the ache away. "I've got ya, sweetheart."

"I'm sick." A worse hacking cough tore through my lungs, burning my throat. I rubbed my nose with the tissue I had balled in my fist, eyes watering.

"I know. I know. We're gonna get ya better. Do ya

want me to sit up?"

Too tired to form words, I shook my head. "Uh eh."

He chuckled. "Okay, sweetie, get some rest."

I must've slept hours on his chest that day, and he didn't move an inch. I'm not sure how old I was. Only that I was in elementary. If I had to guess, I'd say six or seven. Most of the brothers were out on a run. Big stayed behind to care for me since I was sick and everybody knew my mother wouldn't tend to my needs.

It's weird how life works, isn't it? Twenty plus years later here we are dancing in the clubhouse on Christmas Eve. This is the year I fell in love with a man twenty years my senior, had a baby in our house, a party to celebrate her, and countless moments I'll cherish for always.

The song comes to its inevitable close. Instead of letting me go, Big scoops me up like a bride on her wedding night. I squeak in surprise, arms flailing.

"Big, what're you doing?" I slap his pec, laughing.

Five long strides later and I realize exactly what he's up to. As quickly as I go up, I come down on Santa Gunz's lap.

Big winks as he backs away with a devastating smile that melts my heart into a heap of malleable pink putty. He pulls out his cell phone, as does half of the freaking clubhouse full of brothers and their old ladies alike. Jade is here again tonight along with Loretta, White Boy's mom. Don't think I'll ever get over that she's his mother. Beth even brought Jonesy by for a few hours tonight before taking him home and returning to hang with us.

Jizz gives us the thumbs-up.

I can't believe they're doing this to me. My old man of all people.

"Time to get the show on the road, Baby Doll." Gunz drapes my legs over both of his, my ass resting on a thigh. My feet can't touch the ground. Bet all these assholes are loving the show. At least Gunz didn't wear the full costume to play the part. Only a Santa hat and beard. The rest of his outfit is pure Gunz: leather cut, white t-shirt, jeans, shit kickers, and Sacred Sinners belt. Bonez looks more the role than his brother does.

I twist my head to address Mr. Claus. "What show?" We never discussed a show. I should know, I helped plan the night with the sisters.

Gunz winks, smiling beneath that fake, white beard.

What. The. Hell?

"Ho. Ho. Ho. What would you like for Christmas, young lady?" he asks in a deep, Santa-inspired voice.

"Did you just Ho. Ho. Ho. me?"

Gunz pats my thigh. I dunno if it's to calm me or get me to play along with this weird charade. "Why yes, I did, my dear. Now tell me what a beautiful girl like you wants for Christmas?"

Lordy. Alright. Guess we're doing this.

"Come on, Bink. We all wanna know." This comes from Jez who's standing beside Bulk with her phone out. No doubt filming this whole stupid exchange.

I flip her off.

Jizz cracks up. "Now that's no way to act on Christmas, sis, if you don't want coal in your stocking."

Fine.

A-hole.

I flip him the bird as well.

Big snorts, holding back a laugh. I narrow my eyes at him, silently promising a swift and painful death for doing this to me in the first place. The Santa bit and throne was for the kids. Not me.

Bonez reaches around and sets a brightly colored package in my lap. I glare down at the offending thing. "What the shit is this?" I flick the side of the box. Yes, I know this isn't very holly or jolly or even nice of me, but I don't wanna be on everyone's Facebook and Instagram. There's no way they're keeping this to themselves. Bink's humiliation will be the laughingstock of the entire club near and far. Not that I give a crap about that. Payback is a dish best served cold, with a side of *how do ya like me now*?

"It's your gift," Gunz explains.

"What gift?"

"For the white elephant."

"Oh." *Duh.* "Does this mean everybody's gotta sit on your lap, Santa, to get their gift?" If I gotta do it. They do, too. That's fair. What's good for the goose is good for the goddamn gander.

Gunz picks up on my evil scheming right away. "Is that what you want for Christmas?" He squeezes my thigh.

A decisive nod. "Yes, Santa." I tickle his fake beard. It's poor quality. If we do this again next year it'll need an upgrade.

Gunz swishes his hand through the air. "Then it shall be done."

A chorus of groans and "*fucks*" carry through the clubhouse.

"Ha. Ha. Ha, assholes. You thought you were

gonna win this one. Well, guess what, I win!" Both of my arms shoot into the air as I do a small wiggle of triumph on Gunz's lap. I don't give a rat's ass if they film this. Do it. I'm gonna make sure the rest of their Santa experiences are posted alongside mine.

"Can I sit on Bonez' lap instead?" Jez interjects. "Don't want him left out."

Gunz chuckles, shaking his head in pure amusement. I do the same.

Bulk elbows his old lady in the arm. "What the fuck?"

She shrugs like it ain't no thang, massaging the spot he connected with.

Behind me, Bonez laughs. It's deep, sensuous, and sexy as sin.

"Open your present, babe, so you can give the next person a turn." Big juts his chin toward the gift in my lap. Oh. Right. That's a great idea to unwrap these here. Bet a hundred bucks that more than half of whatever's under the tree is naughty. None of us went boring, snore-fest. The funnier, the better. There's a giant bottle of Astroglide and a hundred-count box of condoms from Big somewhere down there. I wrapped a bright green, vibrating cock as mine, since there are more brothers than there are Sacred Sisters. It seemed fitting.

Tearing into the striped paper, I toss the trash onto the floor and pop open the cardboard box the present is in.

Then... I freaking lose it.

They. Did. Not.

Oh my God.

Holding my stomach, I laugh, and I laugh until my muscles ache and tears are dripping. Gunz peers into the box and snickers along with me. Bonez joins in, too, when he sees the goodies inside.

Still laughing, I pull both things out to show everyone.

The first is a Rudolph G-string. If you've never seen one of these before, Rudolph's elongated nose is where a dick goes. It has googly eyes, plush antlers, and a red ball on the tip of the nose, aka tip of the cock. There are thin straps on either side that lead to the floss that fits up a man's butt crack.

Brew hoots and hollers at the silly thing.

A bunch of the brothers smile. Others clap. Some laugh.

Blimp clasps Big on the shoulder. "Looks like you've got a show to put on for Bink tonight, Prez."

Big shoves his hand off. "Fuck off. My dick's too big for that thing. Maybe you should wear it for

Loretta." He's teasing Blimp. There's no malice behind his words. Not when he's smiling from ear to ear, watching me hold Rudolph in the air to give the full effect.

"Big would look hawt in that," Jo throws out. Deke rolls his eyes at his woman.

"I second that," Jez has to add. Bulk covers her mouth to keep her from talking more. Then is disgusted when she licks his palm, but he doesn't release her.

"Third." Candy Cane raises her hand in agreement. What a night. This is hilarious!

The second part of the present is as wild as the first. It's a Rudolph butt plug. More specifically a deer tail attached to a black, tapered plug to match the G-string. You could actually roleplay with this ensemble. Not that we will. But it'll be fun to re-gift next year. Unless I can talk Big into wearing the thing. He's probably right, though. The length of Rudolph's nose is too short for him. Then again, you never know until you try.

As if reading my mind, Big shakes his head on repeat. "Don't even think about it, babe. None of *that* is goin' anywhere near *this*." He gestures to his junk in a circular motion before turning around and doing the same motion to that sexy ass encased in a pair of equally sexy jeans.

He spins back around.

"But—"

Big holds up a hand, cutting me off. "Nope. If I can't fuck your ass, you can't put anything in mine."

I wasn't gonna ask that. But okay. Good to know if I let him, then I can do whatever I want to his back door, too. Turnabout is fair play in this relationship, it appears. I'm cool with that.

I file that notion away to revisit later.

"Okay," I reply, unsure of what else I'm supposed to say. To get this over with I peck Santa on the cheek in thanks, collect my gifts, and join my old man to give someone else a turn to be humiliated in good spirit.

Jez wastes no time strutting up to Santa and taking a seat on his lap. Thus commencing our portion of the adult Christmas party.

She opens a candy cane vibrator provided by Loretta. We all get a good chuckle when she decides to deep throat it for the cameras.

As the night wears on, there's alcohol, various naughty shot glasses, a bag of coal, more sex toys than you can imagine, and a few tamer presents like a poker set and decks of cards that everyone takes turns opening. Nobody fights over things. We get what we get and enjoy ourselves. There's laughter all around. Pictures and videos taken to memorialize the night. Brew passes out drinks. Bottles of Bud or Coors to the men and various mixed cocktails in red Solo cups for us ladies. I don't think I've laughed and smiled this much in years.

Standing in front of Big, sipping on spiked eggnog, my ass to his legs, he wraps his arms around my shoulders as we watch our family take their turns. Bonez gets in on the fun by sitting on his own brother's lap and unwrapping Big's box of condoms and lube. Not leaving Gunz out, they swap places. Gunz puts on his brother's elf hat and surrenders the Santa one so Bonez can look the part. Jez makes lewd comments about the display and begs to get her chance to sit on Bonez's lap. To which, Bulk denies her with a spicy kiss that keeps the wild woman distracted long enough for the brother swap to conclude before she gets herself into more trouble.

Spinning around to face my man, I tap his cheek, grinning at him. "You're up last, sexy."

Big dips down to plant a loud smooch upon my lips. "You got it, Sugar Tits." That dimple is killing me tonight. I dunno if I've seen it this much ever. Nor the twinkle in his eyes. He's happy. From the world of Elizabeth Bennett—incandescently so.

Taking this night in stride, despite his dislike for Christmas, Big takes his half-empty bottle of Bud with him and sits on his sergeant at arms' lap. The amount of space he takes up is comical. You can barely see Gunz beneath Big's massive self. Bonez rests the last present from under the tree on my man's thigh.

Santa doesn't disappoint when he repeats the same speech he has all night, one person after the next. "Ho. Ho. Ho. What would you like for Christmas, Prez?"

Big looks straight at me and lights up the entire common room with his full-fledged smile and flash of pearly whites. My stomach dips at the wonderful sight. Our eyes tether the short distance, and I find myself smiling as wide as him, cheeks aching, insides fluttering, heart thumping to the beat of my love for this man.

Damn, I sound cheesy as fuck.

Big lifts his chin my way and slaps Gunz on the shoulder. "I already got what I want, brother. She's right there."

Oh. My. Bejesus. He's trying to kill me.

I clutch my chest as every single one of the sisters

"aww" a dreamy sigh.

"I love you," he mouths.

"Love you, more," I mouth back, stomach flipping like a schoolgirl with her first crush.

Jizz makes a retching sound in his throat. "Ew. Gross. Get a room, Prez. That's my sister," he teases, thus breaking the romantic spell Big's cast on me. The room erupts into a fit of laughter. Big flips my brother off before he tears into his present with one hand. He pulls out a plush dick and chucks it at Jizz, hitting him in the stomach, not far from his junk. It bounces off and lands on the floor. Pixie picks it up and hands it to me. I hug the soft penis to my chest. It's adorable with its flesh-colored body and beady eyes. There's a white string sewn to the tip, representing cum. So stinking cute. I'm keeping this little guy for sure.

Big and Gunz exchange a few hushed words before the present exchange is concluded. My man stands and throws his wrapping paper in the giant black bag we're using for trash. He drains his Bud and tosses that away too. I meet him halfway between the garbage and where I was standing. One second I'm preparing to wrap my arms around his middle for a much-needed hug. The next, Big's throwing me over his shoulder in a fireman's hold.

Expelling a squeaky laugh, I punch at his ass, my hands full of gifts. G-string and plug in one and the plush peen in the other. "Big, what the hell?"

"Say goodnight, everyone. We've got some fucking to do," my giant asshole declares to the room.

A round of g'nights and Merry Christmases are shared.

Most of the Sacred Sisters sneak around Big so I can see them. They take turns patting me on the back and wishing me Merry Christmas firsthand. I return the sentiment, blood rushing to my head in this position. I try to turn and look at them, but my neck cramps so I give up.

"You ready, babe?" Big spanks my ass hard.

I yelp.

"Put me down. Now! It's not sex time! It's drinking time. Partying time. Not. Sex... Sex later."

Big laughs, it's deep and full of life. The vibrations carry through his shoulder into my stomach.

Hand planted on my bottom, the jerk doesn't say another word as he saunters from the common room, down the stretch of hall, and into his clubhouse bedroom that's still devoid of much more than a bed and a few odds and ends. Kicking the door shut with his boot heel Big drops me onto the bed. I land with a bounce, gifts falling from my hands onto the neatly made bed.

"Big," I grunt on impact, ready to knee him in the gonads.

Ignoring me, Big shucks off his cut and pulls his shirt over his head by grabbing a section of the back and yanking upward. The armholes slide down his biceps until they reach his hands. He discards it and his cut on the foot of the bed.

"Take off your clothes." Big gestures to my fully dressed state with two fingers and a chin lift.

What?

That's not happening.

Like I'm gonna miss this strip show.

Not likely.

It's Christmas Eve. If he wants sexy time, I want the Big show, the whole enchilada. Including the tightly formed abs, he's been working on. Before, he had a nice stomach. Really nice, actually. Now, he's smoking hot. The ridges are sharp, rippling beneath taut, tanned skin that's decorated with ink. Harley's birthday and handprint being his newest addition. Big doesn't have the body of a fifty-one-year-old, that's for damn sure. Those pecs have bulked up more. Brown nipples, continuously hard. The light dusting of hair across his pecs has turned a light gray, as has the small treasure trail down the center of his stomach he let grow. It leads to the sharp V at his hips that's never been this defined before. For all the bitching us chicks do about the brothers' newfound fitness appreciation, we get to reap the benefits. Big has also given up shaving his facial hair daily, so I get a delicious man-candy three-day scruff that turns my crank in the best of ways before he shaves it off again. The handsome man lets it grow for me. I know this. And I love him more for it every day. Just as I love him for everything else he's given me.

"Bink," Big warns, arching an impatient brow when I make no effort to move. His belt buckle flips open.

I rest on my elbows, ankles crossing as they hang over the edge of the mattress.

Big catches on to my game. "You wanna watch?" That sexy pink tongue sweeps across his bottom lip, leaving a sheen in its wake.

My insides quiver, wondering what he's gonna do with that naughty tongue once my clothes are off.

Lips hooking in a private grin, Big pops open the button of his jeans with deft fingers, leaving the zipper intact. The white band of his boxers plays peekaboo from the tiny slit.

"Oh. Yeah. I wanna watch." I nibble my bottom lip so he knows how fucking hot this makes me. My nipples pebble in my bra. Pussy clenches, yearning to be touched.

Big blushes the littlest bit, hiding a schoolboy smile by smashing his lips together. His attention darts away from me to where his thickness is concealed—ready to come out and play.

That's right, baby, your dick's perfect. Come to mama.

"Keep going," I rasp, head lolling to the side as I rake my hooded gaze up and down the fine male specimen that's mine... all mine.

An innocent nod is Big's response a moment before he slowly lowers his zipper, tooth by tooth. Hooking his thumbs into the waistband of his jeans and boxers, he shoves them down his legs in one muscle-undulating swoop. Bent in half, the expanse of his strong back is on full eye-banging display as he undoes his boot laces before returning to his full height. In an adorably shy manner, Big scratches his pec, gaze cast on the floor. That perfect cock sways like a baseball bat above two heavy sacs. My mouth waters, eager to swallow it down my throat... to let him fuck it raw until I can't breathe and tears spill down my cheeks, lips going numb—swollen, well-used.

Jesus.

My man's gorgeous.

I'm the luckiest bitch in the land.

Big takes his time, knowing full well I'm watching this hot-as-sin show. He toes off one boot then the next, leaving nothing but a bit of fabric looped around his ankles.

"Now the pants," I order in a low seductive tone.

"You want me to take off my pants?" He fists his massive erection and pumps it like he has all the time in the world. A clear bead of pre-cum bubbles on the tip. Big uses it as lube to jack himself. A pleased moan battles in his chest as it begins to rise and fall between laden breaths. Needing more pleasure, he cups his balls, squeezing and kneading the sacs until his abs tighten in ecstasy, lips parting to emit a groan.

Fuck. He's killing me.

Teeth sinking into my bottom lip until it hurts, I hum my approval. Then toss the reindeer G-string at his abs where it hits and drops straight to the floor, landing on top of his foot.

"Babe?"

"Please put it on." I want to see him wear it.

A sharp shake of his head, ponytail swaying.

Fine.

Knowing Big isn't gonna do what I want without a little incentive, I scoot to the edge of the bed, slide off my cut and set it atop his. My legs dangle, toes close to touching the floor, as I reach out and wrap my fist around his cockhead. There's plenty of shaft for us to play with together. Silkiness bathes my palm as he growls a string of wanton expletives upon my touch. I use my grip to pull him closer, to get what I really want.

With Big's hand jacking his pole at the base, I quickly remove mine from the tip and swallow his thickness down.

"Fuck!" He shudders, grabbing a fistful of my hair.

I pull off just enough to speak and look up at him. "Fuck my mouth." Pre-cum balms my lips as I trace them with his crown.

The fingers in my hair tighten as does Big's grip on the base of his shaft. "Christ, babe. You sure?" he husks, then swallows thickly, throat working overtime.

To get my point across, I tease his slit with the tip of my tongue, tasting his silky essence, smiling like a wanton club whore. "Yes."

"Hard?"

God. Yes! Make me choke.

I swirl around the crown, flicking the tip to drive him mad. If that's not a yes, I dunno what is.

Big throws his head back. "Fuck!"

"Do it."

Getting his need under control, my man inhales until his chest expands then slaps the side of my face with his spit-soaked shaft, leaving a wet imprint on the exhale. "You're a naughty ol' lady."

"Your old lady."

"Shit yeah, ya are." A growl bellows, nostrils flaring. Big's abs tighten as if he's holding himself back from losing it. Which is what I want him to do. Let go. "So perfect... Are you wet?" he adds.

"What do you think?" I tease, batting my eyelashes.

"Take off your pants."

"No." Not until I get what I want.

Another cock slap to the cheek. "If you want me to fuck that pretty little mouth, you're gonna take off those damn jeans."

"Why?"

"So I can eat your pussy when I'm done using your perfect whore of a mouth." Big hooks his thumb into the corner of said mouth, giving it a slight tug. "Such a pretty place for my dick to claim." A long pause descends as Big looks at me, those baby blues tracing every inch of my face. "Fuckin' Christ, Sugar Tits, how are you real?" My man shakes his head as if he doesn't understand how this is possible. That makes two of us. There was a time in my life I didn't think I'd ever fall in love. Ever feel true soul-transformative pleasure. Then he swooped in and took what he wanted and here we are.

Someone pounds on the door, not giving a damn we're in the middle of something. "We gotta problem, Prez." It's my dad, the club's VP. *Shit.*

Big snarls at the interruption, body going rigid. Our eyes meet. His look equal parts pissed and apologetic. Not sure how that's possible, but he pulls it off. "Yeah, we fuckin' do! I'm with my old lady. This better be end-of-days important, asshole!" Big strokes a knuckle down my cheek and mouths a sincere "sorry." It's amazing how he can be the rudest prick to one person and the sweetest to me in the same breath.

I nod, understanding. This is what you have to get used to when you're the old lady to thee Sacred Sinners prez.

"Run issues. Tacoma," Daddy explains.

"It can't wait thirty?"

"No."

"Fuck! Bring me my goddamn cell."

"Already got it."

"Fine," Big sighs, not in the least pleased. "Open the door with your eyes closed, fuckhead, 'cause you ain't about to see your daughter suckin' my dick. Then back the hell out. I don't wanna see your ugly mug again for the next twelve hours, am I clear?"

I swear I hear my dad chuckle beyond the door a second before it opens. I shut my eyes not wanting to be scarred for life if my father doesn't heed Big's order about keeping those peepers locked down.

There's movement and a gruff, "Now get the hell out," from Big before the telltale snick of the door coming to a close eases the tension in the space.

I breathe a sigh of relief and reopen my eyes one at a time as Big takes the call right where he stands. One hand with the phone, the other threaded through my hair. He positions his still hard prick at my lips and thrusts forward to breach my mouth. I take the tip inside without complaint. If he wants me to play, I'm gonna play, interruption be damned.

"Suck it, babe. It'll make this a lot less fucked up. We aren't losin' momentum *'cause some dumbshits need me to hold their prissy bitch hands.*" Big grates the last bit into the receiver, and I get to work swirling my tongue around his thickness before sucking it deeper into my mouth, growing wetter and wetter the more he fills it, stretching it to the max around his girth like I hope he'll do to my pussy... later.

Flattening both palms atop his thighs for balance, they shiver beneath my touch as Big sets a slow and steady pace of fucking my mouth. Out of respect, I try not to listen to his conversation. Instead, I savor his taste and smooth glide of the velvet steel as it owns me, body and soul.

Three sentences into the conversation and I realize it's gonna be damn near impossible not to overhear bits and pieces when my man's loudly admonishing the sad sucker on the line.

"You don't just lose a shipment. Double check inventory... Did you bring the prospect along?"

Big bottoms out in the back of my throat and rests there, fingernails scraping across my scalp as he peers down at me, appreciating the view with a lazy smirk. My heart punches my breastbone, reveling in the way he looks at me, mouth full of cock. It's not triumphant, it's sincere adoration. Jeez, it's almost sickening how much I care for this man. How much he turns me on, not only physically but emotionally.

How much we fit. Even now when he's on the phone, he's attuned to me and I him.

A heartbeat later our moment's severed when he resumes pumping in and out of my lips and imparting wisdom on a fellow brother. "Dumbasses, the whole lot of ya. How many times I gotta tell ya, Smitty, the boy's green? Did he touch the shipment? – See, that's the problem. Trace the steps. Don't come cryin' to me 'bout this shit. Handle it yourself. I don't care if your prez is gonna put a bullet in one of ya. You should've thought about that before you sent a dumb kid on a run... A dumb kid that shouldn't even be a prospect, to begin with..."

Words fizzle into nothingness as I squeeze my thighs together. A spark ignites there, hot and needy. I unsnap my jeans and shimmy them down my legs, careful not to lose suction on Big's cock.

"Mmmm," I hum around the girth. It twitches as if communicating with its lover.

"*You're killin' me,*" my man mouths, jaw clenching as I scrape the underside of his shaft with my teeth, sending tiny shivers throughout that yummy frame. Even his fingers tremor in my hair and lips part as he ousts a breathy groan, eyes slamming shut. A burst of pre-cum bathes my palate and I swallow it with relish, emitting my own groan steeped with hunger.

He better finish this call soon. We have more pressing matters to attend to... Like this achy pussy of mine that's desperate for his touch. She hasn't gotten proper tongue action in two days. In our sex crazed world, that's a lifetime.

More pumping ensues, in and out in practiced thrusts. Big's eyelids droop, the lines around them accentuating as they focus on me.

"So perfect," he whispers before laying into the jackass intervening on our personal time. "I don't give a flyin' fuck if he was the Pope's son! He's weak. Cut him loose. – What do ya mean what're you gonna do if ya can't find it? You do realize it's Christmas-goddamn-Eve, I have my old lady's sweet lips wrapped around my cock, and I'm *your national prez*. You don't call me for this shit, Smitty. Handle your business."

There's a brief pause from Big as the brother on the line blathers on without taking a breath. I can make out bits and pieces of broken syllables.

When Smitty carries on far too long, Big shuts the inconsiderate bastard down. "Hey! —Yeah. Yeah. You're sorry. You will be when your prez finds out and loses his mind. – No. I ain't tellin' him jack. That's not on me. That's on *you*. You gotta patch for a reason. Man the hell up. And don't call this number again. This is your problem. Fix your shit. Peace." Not waiting a reply Big ends the call with a frustrated growl and chucks his phone to the other side of the bed where it lands on a pillow.

Heaving a sigh, he traces a knuckle down my cheek once more, head shaking in disgust. "Fuckin' morons. Remind me to punch your dad in the dick tomorrow for makin' me handle that bullshit."

I nod, mouth too full of cock to speak. I'll do anything he wants as long as he doesn't stop to punch him now.

"Steel's lucky you're his kid, or he'd be visitin' the shed for the stunt he just pulled. Wanna bet the assholes I call my brothers gave him a hundred for puttin' that on me. They know better. He knows better. Unless someone's dead or in jail, you don't mess with family time." Big's anger isn't blowing over. It's getting worse the longer he stews on the interruption. He's right, though, they know better. And the brothers probably put their VP up to this. They like to razz people for the hell of it. Although, they don't usually include Big in their childish antics since he doesn't like it. But it is Christmas and they're some ballsy motherfuckers when they wanna be. Alcohol has a way of adding extra hair to your chest and bigger cojones below your prick. Come December twenty-sixth they better run for the hills 'cause Big will be gunnin' for them. That, I do not doubt. And I'll be there supporting him the entire way, as I do with most things. We're a team. They mess with him. They mess with me. And the brothers know better than to screw with a Sacred Sister if they wanna eat homemade delights anytime in the foreseeable future. Ask Runner how his screwing over Beth's been working out. Let me fill ya in, it's not.

Redirecting Big's thoughts, I pull off his shaft and lick my lips to stop them from dripping. I place a palm on his abs, staring up at the hottie. "I know, babe. It's over with," I utter softly to ease his temper.

"Yeah." His upper lip snarls, shoulders stiff. A fist clenches down at his side, ready to brawl.

"You can kick their asses soon enough."

"You can fuckin' count on it." A fierce growl.

I chuckle despite his foul mood. "You're sexy, even when you're pissed." To endorse that statement, I gently remove Big's paw from my hair and scoot back on the bed, where I kick the rest of my jeans off. They drop to the ground in front of him as I lean onto my elbows, knees bent, thighs spread for him to dive on in for a taste. Wetness trickles down my slit, in need of attention.

Knowing this lewd display may not circumvent Big's rage, I go for broke and sit up to remove my shirt and nursing bra. The pads inside are almost as soaked as my pussy. I ball the fabric up and toss the pile onto the floor before returning to my elbows, naked save for the striped Christmas socks that reach my knees.

I hook a come-hither finger. "Less thinking, babe. More doing."

Five words and a single gesture is all it takes for my man to snap out of his funk and dive face-first into his favorite treat. There's no hesitation, no room for unnecessary words. He lets his tongue do the talking and what a beautiful poem it creates.

Big lashes my clit, aching to devour me, to fulfill both our desires. So that's what he does... he takes, and he takes—swirling and sucking on that bud until my toes curl and I'm on the brink of losing my mind. A violent shudder washes over me. Pulling a single breath becomes difficult as he consumes my center, growling and feasting like a beast. Two fingers thrust inside my channel. I wail through the torrent of pleasure that blazes like wildfire through every cell. But he doesn't relent. Not for a second. Those digits curl, coaxing my G-spot. My pulse thunders in my throat, my temples, ears. Everything coalesces into a singular spot that beats with the power of a thousand drums.

Then, I'm coming. Hard.

"Fuuuck! Big!" My elbows give out, back falling to the bed as I writhe, screaming through white-hot rapture. He holds me down, arms wrapped underneath my thighs as the current of ecstasy ebbs and flows, only to crash ashore once more when his mouth attacks my clit with renewed vigor. Needing something to hold onto, I grip his hair, nails biting into his scalp as I thrust against his face, desperate for something... anything...

With a hoarse gasp, Big wrenches his lips from my pussy. "Fuck, Sugar Tits," he pants, wiping his damp forehead against my inner thigh to rid the sweat that's gathered there.

"More." I shove his face back where it belongs.

He chuckles at my insistence, then gives me exactly what I desire.

Thank God.

I hiss a throaty "yesss," as his lips encompass my clit.

Taking his job seriously, Big seizes control, and that's all she wrote. Two orgasms turn into three, then four, and by the eighth, I can no longer see straight. Monosyllabic mumblings of my love for him pour like rich maple syrup from my lips as I thrash on the bed, held down by the magician himself.

Number nine explodes like a box of Acme dynamite. My back jackknifes off the mattress, breasts jiggling as they heave toward the ceiling. I dig my heels into Big's shoulders, cursing his unrelenting mouth through the onslaught.

Time ceases to exist.

Breath freezes.

Heartbeat thunders like the hooves of a million horses.

Then, as fast as it came, my climax fizzles, giving way to a warm blanket of contentment. My shoulders collapse against the comforter. I groan, head lolling to the side in exhaustion, eyelids fluttering between open and closed.

No more. I can't take it. Not another one.

Starved of oxygen, I draw in a lungful of air, only to expel it just as quickly. Sweat beads on my brow. Every inch of my skin's over sensitive, muscles twitchy.

Giving me a chance to rest, Big swipes his tongue through my folds, careful not to send me into a convulsing frenzy. "I love you so much," he whispers to my core like she's a person; his breath bathing the most sensitive parts of me with its balming heat. She loves him too, and would tell him as much if she could speak.

Big's ministrations trail lower as he pushes my legs up to sample my untouched rosebud. The sensation's foreign, but not unwelcome.

Around and around he teases the hole as a beastly rumble of delight vibrates in his chest. Seizing the moment, he flicks it with his tongue and pokes the center to breach the outer ring. I moan lightly, enjoying the sensation for it overshadows the throbbing in my hypersensitive clit.

"Big?" I croak, combing my fingers through his now messy hair, body nearly bent in half.

"Humm?" He scoops inside a fraction, and I relax enough to let him explore, not wanting to deter his... fun. He deserves this after all he put up with tonight, even though he detests the holidays.

"Wh—" My voice cracks. I swallow and cough to clear my scratchy throat. "Whenever you're done with that, I want you inside me."

A finger joins his tongue, pressing in deeper, just past the ring. It burns the tiniest bit, but damn if it doesn't feel good. My head tips back, neck elongating as I expel a breath to stave off a moan.

"You have the prettiest ass, babe. I'm gonna get you nice and ready."

"For what?" I brush the backs of my fingers across his sweaty forehead, adjusting to the intrusion.

Big looks up long enough for me to see his face. "The plug." His lips are swollen and a bright cherry red as they capture my soul with that breathtaking smirk of his. The one that promises all the dirtiest things in the world. Sweet Jesus, why's that so hot?

"What plug?" I ask.

Those baby blues glitter with sin. "The one you got for Christmas."

"You want me to wear *that* plug?" My hole clenches around his digit at the thought. I've never done that before. A small part of me is scared to try it, but the mischievous side is beyond thrilled.

"Not want, Sugar Tits. Gonna."

I shiver. "A... a plug."

"Yeah. A plug, in this sweet little hole." To emphasize his statement, Big pushes his finger to the furthest knuckle, deep inside my ass.

Oh... Dear... Fuck...

My eyes tip back into my skull as I fist the comforter on either side of my body, molars clamping down.

"That's it, sweetheart. Right. In. Here." Spitting on my hole to use as lube, Big fingers me there, slow and steady. Every nerve ending flares to life in places I didn't know existed. We may play this way from time to time, but it's rare and never the sole focus. Not like this. Not with him worshiping that forbidden passage.

Keeping the pace, Big moves around on the bed. The scrape of a drawer is opened and pushed closed. There's a *snick*, then refreshing coolness of liquid as it drizzles alongside his digit. He works the wetness inside, coating every inch. A second finger is added with ease. I moan this time, unable to control it, or the pleasure he evokes from places I didn't know could feel this good.

"Big." I reach for him as he kneels between my legs, holding them up to keep me exposed. Taking my hand into his, Big kisses the back with the sweetest kiss before he hooks my arms behind my knees. They touch my shoulders, feet pointing straight in the air, lower back lifted off the mattress.

"There, babe. Hold 'em just like that."

I comply with a nod.

He reaches for the plug that's close to my head and removes his digits from my ass, only to replace the emptiness a moment later with the tip of the toy.

"Push out as I push in," Big instructs.

As uncomfortable as it is, I listen. The rubber stretches my slick hole wider and wider, wedging itself into my virginal back door a little at a time. Big's teeth sink into his bottom lip, attention focused on the task at hand. Those pools of blue expand the deeper he penetrates. I oust a shaky breath feeling every nuance and wanting to experience more. "That's it. Yeah, baby. Suck that plug into your hungry little hole."

I gasp a guttural moan as the biggest portion penetrates my ring, spreading me wider than I've ever been before. Goosebumps sprout from toes to nose, a slight tremor following in their wake.

Oh. Fuck.

I can't believe we're doing this. I can't believe this feels *sooo dammmn gooood.*

My teeth grit together in ecstasy, heart galloping as heat swarms my bottom. Every nerve ending fires off in tandem, blanketing me in acute pleasure that pulses there, delivering signals to my brain—begging for more, more, more.

Big stills, letting the toy's girth continue to stretch me to the max. "You're so open for me, Sugar Tits. So fuckin' beautiful." Unused fingers glide through my dripping folds. Two swirl around the entrance of my cunt before he eases them inside and growls in satisfaction as he massages the thin wall of skin separating my pussy from my asshole. "I can feel it, babe."

"Yeah?" I rasp, expelling a shuddery breath too overwhelmed to form a proper sentence. Nails bite into the backs of my knees, tethering me to this earth before I float away. This is too much. Too intense. Too... It's so tight back there. I'm... *God...*

Big's eyes flare, pupils dilating until the ocean of blue turns to a sea of onyx. He samples his bottom lip with the slow sweep of his tongue. "Yeah, sweetheart," he replies.

With a final push, he inserts the entire plug and scoots back, removing his digits to appreciate the view.

A moan flutters from my parted lips as my asshole hugs the base of the toy, holding it safely inside. Still rock-hard, Big fists his thickness, jacking it in long, practiced strokes, devouring me with those wicked eyes like I'm his last meal. "Proud of you, Sugar Tits. You're goddamn amazing and so fuckin' hot... This ain't gonna last long."

Don't care.

Need him.

Now.

Touching me. Inside me.

Not waiting another second, Big positions himself at my entrance, grips my shoulders for leverage and tears into my pussy like a present on Christmas morning. Slamming to the hilt, air punches from my lungs as his balls collide with the plug... I lose all ability to think, to speak, to do anything more than be his plaything.

Resting my legs on his shoulders, Big jackhammers my pussy with no remorse. I'm a goner. Done. Finito. Ramblings expel from the deepest recesses of my soul as he takes me to a place beyond this world, where pleasure's the only thing that survives. My eyesight fades to blankness as a climax to rival all climaxes rips me in two. It's brutal and it's glorious. I scream, head thrashing amongst the intensity, but it doesn't stop. Nothing does.

"That's it, honey. I love you so much. So fuckin' much. Keep comin' for me, baby."

I do.

I come, and I come. There's no right-side up or upside down. I feel nothing but the intense thrum of ecstasy radiating within my core. Big's heavy breath washes over my face. His sweat drips onto my overheated skin. Growls eject in staccato bursts as his own brand of euphoria drives him closer to the brink of no return.

"Love you," he moans.

In response, I sink my fingers into his biceps to stay connected in any way possible. "Love... you," I somehow force out.

"Fuck. Fuuuck... Gonna... come," he grits, burying himself balls deep. Jets of cum bathe the inside of my pussy as Big peels my legs off his shoulders and collapses on top of me, breathing labored. I wrap my arms around him, legs, too, holding him tight as we float back to reality.

I'm exhausted.

And grateful.

He pecks my temple, chuckling the happiest, tired sound. "Can't believe you're wearin' a plug. That was..."

I twine my fingers through his hair. "Incredible."

Lips drag across my temple before a lazy kiss is pressed upon my cheek, Big's day-old scruff scratching there just how I like. "*You're* incredible. Can't believe this Christmas I got to have my old lady, let alone fuck her like that. You're my match, Sugar Tits. My..." He pauses a beat to catch his breath, as do

I. "The best parts of me. Christ... You're everything."

Turning my head, I nudge him with my chin to get more lovin'. My man props himself up high enough so I can brush my lips across his. "And you're my everything," I whisper against them. "Merry Christmas, my sexy Grinch."

He smiles. "Merry Christmas, Big's Bink. Can't wait to see what gift you give me next year."

Nipping Big's bottom lip, I trace my fingertips up and down his spine. "Next year, you get to wear the plug, hot stuff."

The End... or is it?

Find out what Big does to the brothers on
December 26th by clicking the link below...
BookHip.com/QCFRFH

Readers,

Don't be sad it's over.

The Sacred Sinners have just begun.

Did you squee when I said that?

I hope so...

Because I know a lot of you have been curious about what's next. When is Big's book? Etc... etc...

Yes, I know, it's the end of my original series. One I've enjoyed sharing with you over the course of the last four years. It seemed fitting that the final book is a Christmas one, and published the same week as Vol 1 was all those years ago. What a journey this has been. Hope you agree that this was a grand finale to the series. I downplayed the usual MC drama, so you, as readers, could really get a feel where Big and Bink were at in their lives, what it's like to be a first-time mom, and to finally be at a place where love rules, instead of the constant emotional upheaval. Not that there wasn't a bit of that.

As most of you know, this series is fictional with aspects based in truth. People often ask me if book "Bink" is me. Yes, she is, to an extent. She's brash and ballsy. We look almost exactly the same, apart from tattoos. She doesn't have as many as I do. Nor is she as geeky as I tend to be from time to time. Big *is* a representation of the old man in my life. He's just as much of an asshole, he is much older than me, and those eyes are truly one of my favorite things about him. When I read a few bits and pieces of the Christmas decoration scenes to my real-life Leech, she laughed and commented how accurate that was in our household. #WeLiveWithTheGrinch

It's been a pleasure to share this with you. Parts of my family. My life. And slices that were fun fictional pieces. It's been a blast. Thank you for being a part of it.

Now... the stuff you came here to know more about...

The Sacred Sinners aren't going anywhere... maybe ever. Ya!

If you didn't already know this, you will now... I have a series called Sacred Sinners MC – Texas chapter. I plan to create different chapters this for all the future Sacred Sinners books. MC Chronicles is a diary of sorts only from Bink's POV. Continuing this particular series in another character's voice would take away what I want people to learn and embrace from the series and Bink. So... without further ado... The series that will cover all your favorite people from MC Chronicles will be titled Sacred Sinners MC – Mother Chapter. When the first book will be released, I haven't quite decided that as of yet. But it is for sure on the books. At this point, I've got at least four titles pinned down to write in that series. Possibly more. Depending on what I cook up with the brothers. They have a way of deciding for me as time goes on.

Again, thank you for reading.

Peace, Bink

P.S. Don't forget to post your review on Amazon when you're through. It would mean the world to me.

16830956R00079

Made in the USA
Lexington, KY
18 November 2018